Antoine's name escaped her lips

Suddenly Kate was thrust aside, and Charles's eyes blazed down at her with an inexplicable fury. Her senses reeling from his kisses, she was unaware that she'd murmured aloud her brief pitying thought for the man she was to have married.

"Antoine! Did you call his name when I was making love to you?" Charles demanded.

"No, I...." Deprived of the support of his arms, Kate fell back miserably. "Charles..." she sobbed, her hands outstretched appealingly.

"No! I won't be a surrogate lover for anyone—not even my dear cousin, Antoine!" His dark gaze roamed contemptuously over her disheveled clothing, her heaving bosom. "We'll simply have to forget this sordid episode ever occurred."

The next moment he was striding angrily away, leaving her trembling with despair....

WELCOME
TO THE WONDERFUL WORLD
OF *Harlequin Romances*

Interesting, informative and entertaining,
each Harlequin Romance portrays an appealing
and original love story. With a varied array
of settings, we may lure you on an African safari,
to a quaint Welsh village, or an exotic Riviera
location—anywhere and everywhere that adventurous
men and women fall in love.

As publishers of Harlequin Romances, we're
extremely proud of our books. Since 1949,
Harlequin Enterprises has built its publishing
reputation on the solid base of quality and
originality. Our stories are the most popular
paperback romances sold in North America; every
month, six new titles are released and sold at
nearly every book-selling store in Canada and the
United States.

A free catalogue listing all Harlequin Romances
can be yours by writing to the

HARLEQUIN READER SERVICE,
(In the U.S.) 1440 South Priest Drive, Tempe, AZ 85281
(In Canada) Stratford, Ontario, N5A 6W2

We sincerely hope you enjoy reading
this Harlequin Romance.

Yours truly,

THE PUBLISHERS
  Harlequin Romances

Cast a
Tender Shadow

by

ISABEL DIX

Harlequin Books

TORONTO • LONDON • LOS ANGELES • AMSTERDAM
SYDNEY • HAMBURG • PARIS • STOCKHOLM • ATHENS • TOKYO

Original hardcover edition published in 1981
by Mills & Boon Limited

ISBN 0-373-02491-6

Harlequin Romance first edition August 1982

CHAPTER ONE

THE nightmare varied only in detail; the essentials were always the same. She stood listening to the wedding service, the gauzy veil covering her face, the comforting touch of his fingers on hers. The words were eternal, moving whatever the language, and although they were being spoken in a tongue with which she had only a short acquaintance, in her mind she was hearing the beautiful age-old ones from the Book of Common Prayer.

She knew enough French to be able to respond at the proper places, and it was only when they moved into the vestry of the tiny church that the horror began. For when the bridegroom raised the veil from her face to kiss her, she looked not at Antoine, but into the eyes of a total stranger.

Kate Ellerdale woke with a start, her pitiful sobbing stifled by the cover which she pressed against her mouth while her wide bewildered gaze flitted round the luxurious sun-drenched bedroom. Instinctively the slender hand moved from her mouth to wipe the stinging tears from her cheek. She gave a shuddering sigh of relief that she was awake, that she had escaped from that repetitive horrible dream, but still her eyes moved restlessly about the room in a desperate search for the reassurance she sought.

The bedroom *was* familiar, and yet . . . She knew that wall of cupboards whose light wood doors concealed enough space for the clothes of the Queen of England. Then on that dressing-table she could see her own jars and bottles, the pretty pink and navy make-up bag she had bought before she left London. And through the slightly open doorway on the opposite wall the exotic gold and pink tiles of the bathroom could just be glimpsed and she knew that she had bathed there more than once in recent days. Then total recollection flooded back, clouding the brilliance of the violet eyes and causing the white teeth to catch painfully at the trembling lower lip.

It was true, then. The nightmare was more than a sleep-disturbing dream, it was a haunting reality, one which had been with her for almost a week. Since that day in church when, after the wedding service, she had realised that she was married to the wrong man. To someone she had never seen before in her life.

It had all begun so romantically, so idyllically two months ago in England. She had been catapulted from the relatively humdrum, rather boring routine of photographic modelling to the infinitely more exciting and certainly more glamorous world of high fashion. A friend of a friend had introduced her to Kulukundis, the brilliant young Greek designer who had arrived like a comet blazing across the London scene. And the very next morning he had rung her suggesting that she might care to model his next collection.

Of course Kate had been suspicious, for even in the short time he had been in the public eye Kulu had established a reputation second to none in a world where almost anything goes. And when she had mentioned at that morning's photograph session that she had a date with Kulu there had been one or two rather snide references to the 'casting couch'. Beverley Ann Davies had been particularly scathing.

'Well, so you're going to give in at last, Katie dear.' There was no mistaking the sour envy in the voice, no escaping the discontented droop that marred the beautiful mouth as she surveyed her colleague in the mirror in the tiny dressing-room they shared.

'No.' Over the past two years Kate had learned that the only way to deal with bitchiness was to ignore the little barbs. 'It's purely a business meeting, Beverley Ann. Dear!'

'I bet.' The tall blonde girl leaned back against the wall, watching Kate struggle out of the skin-tight motor-cycle gear which had featured in a hairspray advertisement, then stand for a moment in pants and bra fiddling with the zip of a muslin dress which she was to wear for the vermouth feature. 'You know, you'll have to watch your figure, Katie. You're putting on a pound or two of weight, and from what I hear Kulu insists on absolute Twiggys to wear his clothes.'

Momentarily shaken from her musing thoughts, Kate turned to glance in the mirror. 'Do you think so, Beverley?' She put an anxious hand to the firm swell of her breast while she twisted about, studying her reflection anxiously.

'Yes.' There was a hint of triumph in the other girl's smile. 'You're looking almost . . . well, buxom, I suppose the word is. Mind you,' she made a pretence of comforting, 'although he likes his models to be laths, there's no saying what Kulu's personal preferences are.

After all, he's used to Greek women and they're inclined to be—well covered.'

So when Kate, in a state of some alarm, presented herself at Kulu's flat for the interview, she scarcely knew whether to be relieved or piqued that his interest in her was so professional, without even the most oblique suggestion that he had the casting couch in mind.

'Yes,' he decided, chewing on a long black cigar, 'I like the way you move. You've studied ballet, I guess.' And when Kate admitted that she had gone to classes for many years he nodded approvingly. 'Good. It's time you English girls realised that cool elegance isn't enough. But anyway, you'll do.' With a wave of a languid hand he dismissed her. 'Fix terms through your agent and come along next week. We've a lot of work to do and I'm not prepared to put up with poor work or bad time-keeping.'

And Kate found herself out on the doorstep, smiling ruefully at the idea that she had gone there prepared to fight for her honour if necessary. Later, when she had started work for Kulu, she learned that he was for the moment obsessed with a long-legged redhaired Texan and presumably all his energies were expended in trying to bring her to heel. Or to bed, more likely.

Working with Kulu was a challenge that no girl could ignore, and Kate revelled in the exquisite clothes which were shown to buyers from all over the world and in glamorous settings such as she could have scarcely imagined. It was against the background of a famous stately home in Dorset that she first met Antoine, and strangely that evening, when his dark eyes were making her blush with their blatant admiration as she whirled or drifted along the catwalk, she had the fleeting sensation that somewhere she had seen him before. There was something vaguely but persistently familiar about the set of his head, the dark, almost black eyes, almond-shaped under thin dark eyebrows. But that was impossible, for he later said that his appearance here was simply by chance, that he had come along to the fashion show to support the charity for which it was being held that particular evening, and because a friend who had found at the last moment he had another engagement had given him the ticket.

When the show was over, the girls, wearing their own Kulu clothes which were sold to them at cost, were allowed to mingle with the guests. Katie, wearing glowing cotton voile in shades of violet and mauve, found herself talking with a group of the international jet-setters who appeared to make up the majority of the audience, responding, with the veneer of sophistication she had cultivated so assiduously, to the flattery of the men who gravitated in her direction.

She was laughing at a joke made by a tall middle-aged man in the dazzling white robes of an Arab, sipping a glass of champagne, when she realised that the man she had noticed so persistently during the show was at her side. She felt his eyes, the ones that seemed so vaguely familiar, rake her profile with an intense intimate glance and when he spoke there was no procrastination.

'It is so warm, *mademoiselle*.' The accent was foreign as she had known it would be, although his command of English was almost perfect.

'Yes.' She turned towards him, violet-blue eyes encouraging him over the rim of her glass. 'Yes.

Such a beautiful evening.'

'Shall we walk on the terrace?'

'That would make it perfect.'

Together they stepped out through the floor-length window close to where they had been standing, out into the darkening world, all the noise, chatter and brilliance of the great house seeming to drift away from them. As if they alone were real, all the others shadows, thought Kate dreamily. They didn't speak but walked the length of the house, their feet moving soundlessly over the mellow old paving stones towards the balustraded edge of the terrace and the flight of shallow steps leading down to the rose gardens. They stood silently savouring the soft scents of the warm evening, the spicy musk of rose and dianthus, the faint sweetness of a laburnum tree as its golden flowers faded and fell on to the sun-hot stones. Then, turning to her, he took the glass from her hand, placing it beside his on the stone balustrade close to where they stood. And he kissed her.

Soon they were so wildly in love that their constant, wondering questions about the coincidence of that first meeting ceased to amaze. It had nothing to do with Antoine's friend who couldn't use the ticket and was all to do with fate which had guided him along an inevitable path. So they assured each other as they wandered blissfully through the London parks and gardens during the warm evenings of that everlasting summer. And Kate knew with perfect simplicity that she had never been so happy in her life.

It was sheer tragedy and disaster when the time came for Antoine to return to France, when the business of negotiating the wine contracts which had kept him in London came to an end. Even while she kept assuring herself that France wasn't so very far away, she had the feeling that the remote part where Antoine's family had their château and vineyards was much more cut off than the rest of the country. That much she had deduced from certain things he had told her about his life there.

But even that was to be no obstacle, for on the very last evening, after they had dined in a smart little French restaurant, he proposed to her. They were walking along Park Lane, hearing the whispering swish of a light breeze moving through the leaves high above their heads, pausing to kiss as they were so constantly impelled to do. And then he asked her.

'Oh, Antoine!' There was a glitter of tears on her long lashes as she looked at him, but for the moment she seemed incapable of further speech.

'Come, *chérie*.' The dark boyish face teased as he looked down at her. 'Surely this is no time for crying?'

'I'm not. At least . . . It's just that I'm so happy.'

'That's logical. Feminine but logical.' The hands circling her waist tightened, his expression grew serious. 'Does that mean your answer is yes?'

'Of course!' She reached her hands round his neck and brushed her mouth against his. 'I shouldn't have thought you would need to ask.' Her voice had grown husky.

'But I do.' For a moment she thought a shadow, a brief fleeting look of uncertainty passed over his face, but it was so vague that it was probably some trick of the lights cast briefly over them from the passing traffic. 'I do, my sweet. A girl like you . . . Oh, I do.' And his face came down to hers, kissing her with a passion that left her breathless.

And that was the end of their wild impetuous courtship, for the very next morning he flew back to his home with her firm promise that she would follow in a month's time and that they would be married as soon as she arrived.

'Don't forget, my love,' his farewell kiss had been full of an aching sadness which only later did she begin to understand, 'don't forget that I adore you. Whatever happens . . .'

'Don't say that!' In a sudden unexpected gesture of fear Kate laid her face against his chest, wrapping her arms tightly about him. 'Oh . . .' she gave a tremulous apologetic little laugh, '. . . say you adore me. But nothing's going to happen.' She looked up into his face with a determined smile. 'Nothing is going to happen.' She repeated the words in a whisper that excluded all the busyness of the great airport. 'Except that you and I are going to marry soon, and live happily ever after.' Her eyes searched the dark handsome features as she tried to imprint each detail on her memory. 'I hope, Antoine, that your mother won't be against our marriage.' Something about the way he had spoken gave Kate the impression that his mother would be a very formidable woman who always managed to get her own way.

'Of course she will not. When she sees you she will love you as much as I do.' A faint smile touched his mouth. 'Almost as much as I do.' Kate searched his face again, and when his plane had eventually taken off she wished she could rid herself of the idea that he was much less confident than his words suggested.

But when a month later Kate flew out to Lyon for her wedding, she had almost forgotten her misgivings.

Certainly it was discouraging that she had been met at the airport by the chauffeur instead of Madame Savoney-Morlet or by Antoine's stepsister Bernice. Antoine she had not expected as he had suddenly had to fly off to Hamburg.

'But,' he had assured her over a crackly line the previous day, 'I shall be back as soon as possible. And certainly in time for the wedding.'

Only the drive through the wet cold grey French countryside behind the silent sullen-looking chauffeur was not the welcome Kate had expected. Neither was this the France she had expected. She shivered a little as they climbed out of Le Puy by a road that twisted, giving wide, constantly changing views of a bleak landscape interrupted by weird volcanic contortions almost like deformities.

The light was beginning to go by the time they turned off the road, driving for what seemed like miles along a twisting path shrouded by high bushes before finally turning through the gates which proclaimed to the world the importance of the Savoney-Morlets. With a sigh of relief Kate sat forward on her seat as the limousine came to a halt in front of the great house, looking in vain for a door being thrown open in welcome, even the twitch of a curtain that would have shown that someone inside was interested in her arrival.

Madame Savoney-Morlet was darker than her son and so lacking in charm that try as she would Kate could see no resemblance between them. She was older than the woman Kate had expected, with a wrinkled face which heavy make-up and dark lipstick did little to improve. The eyes were deep-set and brilliant under drooping lids that gave the face a watchful, slightly sinister appearance that Kate found chilling.

'*Mademoiselle*.' Kate, standing in the centre of the hall where she had been left by the maid, stared at the intimidating figure and felt her hand taken in a brief reluctant grasp. Then as she turned to lead the way into the salon Madame embarked on such a torrent of rapid French that the girl was totally lost.

'I'm sorry, *madame*,' even the most simple words seemed to have fled her brain, 'I'm just beginning to learn your language, but have not made much progress so far.'

Madame turned to stare at her for a moment, then as if realising there was nothing to be gained by a one-sided conversation she began to speak in heavily accented English.

'So, *mademoiselle*.' Madame poured some very weak tea and handed a cup across the marble table where Kate was perched on the edge of an uncomfortable chair covered in faded damask. 'My son tells me you are a mannequin.' Disapproval showed in every line of her face.

'Yes.' Kate sipped the tasteless cool liquid. 'That's how we met—at Werne Abbas Manor,' she added, hoping the name of the famous house would impress her hostess.

'And you have parents?' Madame showed no sign of having heard of Werne Abbas.

'Yes.' A tiny hint of defiance crept into Kate's voice as she made up her mind that there was nothing to be gained by allowing Antoine's mother to dominate her completely. Obviously she was a bully, and the only way to deal with bullies is to stand up to them. So she had been told! She swallowed, trying to control her nervousness. 'As I told you in my letter, *madame*, I have a mother and a stepfather. Unfortunately they are travelling in South America at the moment and I cannot contact them.'

'And it is usual in England,' Madame's thin arched eyebrows almost reached the black hairline, 'it is usual in England for girls to marry without their parents' advice or permission?'

'Not usual.' Kate put down her cup with a trembling hand. 'But I am of an age to decide these things for myself.' Not for the world would she have admitted to this cold unfriendly woman that her marriage plans had that hint of the clandestine which her romantic nature had always sought and which circumstances had obligingly provided. Only now was the cold hand of doubt clutching at her heart. But as she stared at the woman opposite she saw a slightly amused, almost smug expression pass over her features. It was a look Kate could not understand but one which caused her some trepidation.

'Then I shall have you shown to your room, *mademoiselle*.' A jewelled hand went out to press a concealed button under the table and the unfriendly features were impassive again. 'If there is anything you want then please ask one of the maids.'

'Oh please,' impulsively Kate leaned forward to smile at the other woman, 'can't you call me Kate? After all, as we're to be so closely related . . .'

'*When* you are my son's wife, then we shall adopt a more familiar form of address.' Again there was a flicker of satisfaction on Madame Savoney-Morlet's face. 'Until then . . . In France at least we prefer to adhere to the formalities.'

'Of course.' The reproof and the condescending manner she adopted brought the shaming colour flooding into Kate's cheeks and she sat with her head bowed, her fingers fumbling with her handbag until she heard the door behind her open and the maid, summoned by the bell, come inside. She heard the rapid conversation and knew that orders were being given about the guest being taken to her bedroom. Kate stood up, a great weariness making her legs feel weak and sluggish.

'And Antoine . . .?' Miserably she looked at the woman, willing her to relax just a little. 'Is there no chance of seeing him this evening, *madame*?'

'No.' There was the merest hint of a thaw in the woman's manner. 'No, it is not usual. Besides, as you know, at the moment he is away from home attending to an important business matter. It is a pity . . .' she shrugged, '. . . but this evening at dinner you will meet my stepdaughter and a few friends, so we shall at least have some company. Besides, you have not long to wait till the wedding. Do not concern yourself, *mademoiselle*.' The mouth smiled, the brilliant eyes were blatantly mocking. 'Assuredly Antoine Charles will be waiting for you when you reach the altar tomorrow.'

As she followed the maid across the wide lofty hall, Kate had the impression that somehow time had moved more slowly in this part of Europe than in the places she knew. The château, although splendid enough to satisfy the most exacting historian, was scarcely a home, with its crumbling stone walls, and there was no sign of anything having been acquired, even in the name of comfort, for the last hundred years.

Even the maid, with her black dress and stockings, the dated frilly white cap and apron, looked as if she

had escaped from some musical comedy of the thirties
—although the severe expression surely would have
made her unsuitable for any part in such a show.

For the first time Kate wondered if it was in fact
such a romantic thing to live in a château. The word
had always conjured up a more inviting elegant picture
than the English equivalent, and she had never yearned
to live in a castle. And yet this enormous crumbly
place with its long stone corridors and high ceilings,
the coldness of the black and white marble, was unlike
anything she had imagined. The sundrenched warmth
was missing, she decided with a spasm of homesickness
for the sunny warm city she had left, the warm courtyards buzzing with heat-mazed insects . . .

Her musings were brought to an abrupt end when
the maid stopped at the end of the endless corridor and
threw open a heavy wooden door, standing aside so that
Kate could go ahead.

'Thank you.' For a moment she stood just inside the
door, looking round the melancholy room, then she
turned, some query hovering on her lips as she tried to
find the right words. But the door closed with a firm
click.

The room was large and on the high vaulted ceiling
biblical scenes were painted, the kind that might have
been suitable in a church or concert hall but which Kate
knew she would not enjoy lying in bed looking at. Not
that such a thing would be possible, she decided, for
once she was ensconced in the enormous bed, the side-
curtains and hangings would exclude almost everything else. She wondered if she and Antoine would
have to share this room, this bed, when they were
married. And would their lovemaking be inhibited by

the knowledge that the Angel Gabriel and his friends were spying on them? She shivered, and then laughed at her fanciful imagination.

The walls of the room had been covered with silk that once had been green but which now had lost all its original colour. The curtains and drapes were of a heavy dull green material and the furniture was dark and massive.

With a sigh Kate wandered across to the window and looked out at the lowering clouds and the sad dripping rain. Even the weather seemed determined to make what ought to have been the most exciting time of her life gloomy and forbidding. She felt an urge which she had experienced downstairs, a longing to have her mother with her, for the utter conventionality of a normal wedding in England with her friends and relatives about her.

The words of her flatmate came back to her, words that had annoyed Kate when Hilary first expressed them.

'Are you sure you're doing the right thing, Kate? To me it wouldn't seem like a wedding without my family around me.'

'But can't you understand, Hilary, that's exactly what I love about it. I always swore I'd have a different sort of wedding, you know that.'

'Well, I only hope . . .' Hilary had been annoyingly doubtful. 'After all, you don't know Antoine so very well, do you?'

'Well enough to know that he's the only man I could ever marry.' There was a flush of anger on Kate's cheeks. 'Oh, and,' she gave a little laugh, determined not to let Hilary know how wounding her words had been, 'if you're worrying about being done out of a wedding, then stop. After we've been to Greece for our honeymoon, Antoine says we're going to have a huge party at the Savoy, and of course you'll be one of the most important guests. By that time Mum and Andrew should be back to civilisation.'

'I expect your mother will go berserk. I know mine would.' Hilary spoke with the smugness of a girl whose mother still sent a parcel of food regularly from Yorkshire in case her daughter wasn't eating enough.

'My mother has always trusted me.' Even as she spoke Kate wondered if that were really true. Or was it simply that she was more interested in her new husband than the daughter she had had for twenty years? And had Kate herself a dubious motive for embracing the hasty wedding plans with such enthusiasm? Was she perhaps trying to repay the hurt she had suffered six months ago when the cable had come from New York?

'Andrew and I married this morning,' it had read. 'Lyrically happy. Writing soon. Love, Mother.'

And then a week later had come the airmail letter, full of crinkly white paper covered with writing in large round characters.

'So you'll understand, darling,' the letter had ended, 'it was all so much of a hurry. Andrew couldn't afford to miss the chance of this trip to Ecuador and wanted me to go with him. That meant getting married so as not to shock the faculty. We'll be away eight months, and then you're to come and stay as long as you like.'

Kate had tried to hide her feelings under a thin covering of bitter amusement. The thought of her mother, who loved cities, scented baths and good food,

spending months on an archaeological dig somewhere
in the wilds of South America! Yes, amusement was a
very sound defence against the hurt. And now, surely
her mother could hardly complain when she had done
the very same thing. And after all, Kate didn't even
have an address where she could be easily contacted.
'In any case,' she assured Hilary as much as herself,
'you must admit that Antoine is the kind of man that
most mothers dream about—good-looking, rich and
with a château,' she finished with an attempt at humour.

'Hmm.' Hilary sounded so doubtful that the only
conclusion Kate could draw was that her friend was
just a little bit jealous. 'Yes, well, there are châteaux
and châteaux,' she said cryptically.

Kate gave a weak little smile as she turned from the
window and towards the green sub-aqueous gloom of
her bedroom. At least there was no doubt about the
château, it was the only word that could be used with
such a place. Those huge metal gates, the crest picked
out in gold and two savage snarling stone greyhounds
guarding the entrance from the tops of the pillars
belonged to no ordinary residence. But, she gave a
shuddering little sigh, she would have given anything
to find herself in one of those pleasant little villas which
they had passed on the way from the airport.

At dinner that night the party was enlivened as
Madame had promised by Antoine's half-sister Bernice
and two elderly married couples, neither of whom
spoke English and who gave the impression of being so
much in awe of Madame and their auspicious sur-
roundings that they spoke very little French either.

The dining room to which they were guided when
the meal was announced was no more welcoming than

the rest of the place, and Kate wondered if there was something special about the house which defied all attempts to lighten it. For this room, which at first gave the impression of over-illumination with six-branched candelabra marching down the length of the long highly polished table while overhead a crystal chandelier hung with dozens of glowing bulbs, in fact seemed to have an inherited gloom. In spite of the mirror-lined walls where the lights were reflected time and again, to Kate's slightly feverish imagination there was something shadowy, slightly sinister about the room.

Perhaps it was the people, thought Kate, taking her place on the left of Madame Savoney-Morlet at the top of the table, for men and women alike were dressed in lugubrious black. Only her own dress in sapphire blue chiffon brought a glow of colour to the gathering, and Madame's look of disapproval when Kate came downstairs had indicated clearly enough her feelings on the matter. It would have been hopeless for Kate to explain that she had chosen the dress because it was Antoine's favourite and that even at this last minute she was hoping he would sweep into the room, bend low over her chair and kiss her cheek—in front of all of them, assuring them all that this was the girl he was going to marry in the morning. And assuring Kate herself.

And then later, when they had the opportunity to be alone for a moment, he would whisper that the colour still matched her eyes as it had done in London. And when he took her to her room he would whisper, 'Bonsoir', in an impatient lover's tone, remind her that this time tomorrow they would be in their Paris hotel with weeks of love on a Greek island ahead of them.

Tears stung her eyes when she realised how futile it was to expect him to come tonight, but she blinked furiously when she realised that Madame was speaking to her.

'I'm so sorry, *mademoiselle*, that none of our guests speak English.' Her eyes travelled with complacency over the four submissive guests before her gaze briefly returned to the dazzling face of the girl by her side. 'We are such a remote little community. You must make do with myself and Bernice.' She laughed briefly, harshly, and Kate looking quickly round the table saw the guests smile nervously, with no sign of understanding.

'That is all right, *madame*.' She was grateful for the sympathetic smile of Antoine's half-sister who sat opposite. 'I hope to learn the language quickly so that I shall be able to fit in with the family. I did begin lessons after Antoine left, but life was slightly hectic and I didn't make as much progress as I intended. It's a pity that at school I learned Spanish when French would have been so much more sensible.'

'You will learn quickly enough.' Bernice smiled in her shy nervous way with a brief apologetic glance at her stepmother. 'When you have to use it for shopping and running your household and . . .'

'*Oui*.' Madame concluded the conversation by pushing her chair back firmly and murmuring a few words which the guests clearly understood as an invitation to return to the salon where coffee would be served, and there they sat in chairs pulled round to the window through which they could look out on a small enclosed courtyard. The rain had stopped and a faint haze hung low over the ground as if at last it was beginning to dry out.

'There.' Madame Savoney-Morlet turned to Kate, pointing to the glass with the cheroot she was smoking through a long tortoiseshell holder. 'There we shall have the wedding repast tomorrow.' Her laugh was devoid of amusement, showing large, slightly yellow teeth. 'The long tables and chairs are all ready in the passages next to the kitchen. All we must wish for is a fine day.'

'Yes.' Kate looked out on the dreary scene, trying to feel pleased that the rain had stopped. 'But what if it isn't a fine day?'

'Ah, if it rains.' Again that mysterious complacent look flitted over the woman's face. 'If it rains then you will be all the more anxious to go off on your wedding journey.' The dark eyes noticed the blush as it spread across the girl's cheeks and she laughed, saying something in rapid French that made her obedient guests join in her amusement.

Soon the visitors, perhaps interpreting a signal from their hostess, declared that they must go, and after much bowing and thanks to Madame for the great honour she had shown in inviting them to the château, they were shown out by the maid. Madame followed them into the hall and from there the noise of their departure echoed back into the salon, Madame's strong tones dominating the conversation. Bernice and Kate were left alone for a few moments and the older girl leaned forward with a friendly expression. She was a plain middle-aged woman who gave every sign of being completely under the thumb of her stepmother.

'I am so happy you are joining our family.' Her accent was more difficult to follow than her mother's, her command of English less. 'I think Antoine Charles is indeed fortunate.'

Kate's heart warmed. 'Thank you, Bernice.' She smiled, suddenly radiant at the thought of being married to Antoine tomorrow. 'You all call him Antoine Charles . . .?'

'Ah, that is to distinguish one from the other.' As she spoke the strident tones of Madame Savoney-Morlet could be heard approaching and she came into the room in time to hear the last part of what Bernice had been saying. Suspiciously she looked from one to the other before releasing a torrent of questions at her stepdaughter, clearly demanding an explanation of their brief discussion. Her eyebrows came together in a sudden frown.

'*Oui*. But now, *mademoiselle*, you will come upstairs and I will show you the wedding veil.'

'But . . .' Kate shook her head in silent protest, 'I'm not wearing a veil. It's just a simple dress. And I decided to wear a hat with it, a floppy picture hat. It's in that large round box and there are flowers to one side.' She smiled at her own confusion, looking in vain for a response in the face of the woman opposite. 'The flowers are on the hat, not the box and . . .' The words trailed away as Madame shook her head emphatically.

'That will not do. Come.' She strode towards the door with her emphatic manner.

Kate looked appealingly at Bernice, who only shrugged slightly, then shook her head deprecatingly. So she had no choice but to follow the older woman across the hall and up the shallow curved staircase where all the ancestors of the family looked down on them.

'You will see, *mademoiselle*,' the thin claw-like hand

was waved in the direction of a portrait which hung in a dimly-lighted alcove, 'all the Savoney-Morlet brides have worn the family veil.' Kate looked at the pale features of the young woman dressed in Edwardian fashion, then at another earlier portrait, as they turned on to the main corridor. Both brides were wearing, thrown back from their faces, the family heirloom referred to, a fine silk veil, richly embroidered with elaborate panels of flowers and birds and held on top of the head with a high coronet of pearls.

It would, thought Kate, quite spoil the simple lines of the lovely dress which Kulu had made specially for her, and her first instinct was to refuse quietly but firmly to conform to the tradition. This instinct was reinforced when she saw that the veil which had been laid out on the bed in her room had yellowed with age and would look dowdy, dirty even against the sheer white of her dress. But when Madame seemed to expect no resistance Kate gave a metaphoric little shrug of her shoulders. In the interests of family tranquillity it was a small enough price to pay. If she could soften her mother-in-law's harsh attitude towards her then she would give in and wear the veil. But, and she was to learn this only when it was too late, in a dimly lit ancient church such a voluminous, heavily embroidered veil could make a very effective screen.

It was strange next day driving in the same limousine which had collected her from the airport, the same withdrawn chauffeur at the wheel and with Madame Savoney-Morlet by her side. Madame who was to give her away, who would so dearly like to do exactly that but who instead was obliged to receive her into the family. Strange . . . Kate bit her lip fiercely and turned away, looking out at the dullness of the dry day.

At the end of this ordeal would be Antoine. Antoine. Her anguish disappeared as she thought of his arms about her, his mouth on hers. Antoine. Soon she would feel her hand enclosed in his and she would know that she was safe.

'Come, *mademoiselle*.' The firm, not-to-be-questioned voice cut into her reverie and the severe features did not soften as Kate turned appealing eyes to her. At the same time the car came to a halt at the bottom of a flight of steps and following them Kate saw the small church at the top of an eminence.

She counted twenty as she climbed, Madame Savoney-Morlet's firm grasp on her elbow allowing her to devote her attention to keeping the hem of her dress clear of the steps. Couldn't they, she wondered mutinously, couldn't they, one of the servants, have swept the steps for their wedding day? At the top they paused and Madame actually smiled as she reached up to pull the heavy folds of the veil about the girl's face.

'Antoine Charles will have a very beautiful bride.' And she turned, offering her arm to Kate, then led her into the church.

The old priest dressed in vestments all white and rich with gold smiled and nodded his way through the service, and Kate was moved, entranced by all its beautiful strangeness. The heavy scent of arum lilies in the tall crystal altar vases mingled with the incense dispensed through the small circular church from the swinging censer. It *was* the exotic, the unusual wedding her romantic imagination had always craved, here in this tiny private chapel of a French château, without a single guest whom she knew. What could be more unusual or romantic! All her doubts were swept away as if they had never existed.

Her hand was closely linked in Antoine's. She stole a tiny sideways glance at him, her view made shadowy and mysterious by the folds of the heavy enveloping veil. She could just distinguish his dark profile against one of the high windows set into one of the thick medieval walls.

How tall he was—taller even than she had remembered. And he was wearing a different cologne. With a burst of tender recollection she remembered teasing him about his scent when he was in London, for he had worn a very popular and fiendishly expensive fragrance which she told him he was the third of her boy-friends to use. He had been a little piqued at the information, but obviously he had not forgotten. This new cologne was subtle and sophisticated, faintly spicy with a hint of the Orient. Her grip on his fingers strengthened and the strong response made her catch her breath with an ecstasy of love and joy.

A moment later they were walking away from the high altar towards the tiny vestry, she was signing her name, Kate Ellerdale, for the last time. Twice she signed, once for the priest and again to conform to the civil requirements, just as Antoine had told her. Then and only then did he bend towards her, lifting the folds of the veil from her face as he did so, smiling faintly as if he were amused by the performance he had just given. And Kate was searching that face which was so like Antoine's, the face that she had never seen before in her life. Only the swelling notes of the organ drowned the sobbing cry that burst from her lips as his mouth came towards hers.

CHAPTER TWO

'Be quiet, Kate.' The words, though softly spoken, were brusque, a compelling command at the same moment as his mouth came down to quash the cry that rose to her lips. Beyond them, the organ, magnificent and powerful for so small a church, continued to thunder majestically. 'If you want to do what is best for Antoine, don't say a word.' His manner was imperative enough to stifle the distraught protest that sprang to her pale lips. His hands tightened like any other bridegroom's and he smiled down at her, exerting his will by sheer magnetism as the gentle old priest came forward, peering shortsightedly, and he was followed by Madame whose eyes swept over Kate's colourless cheeks then looked into her eyes with the naked triumph she had been struggling to conceal.

Kate heard the man she had married speak to the priest, her hand held securely while a few more words of blessing were murmured over them both. The floor and walls were spinning about her head and only his arm about her waist kept her from slipping to the ground. Then to the swell of organ music they were walking down the central aisle through the small groups of smiling guests and servants who clustered about laughing and shouting congratulations.

Several times Kate heard the name Antoine Charles,

28

but she stood without once glancing at the man by her side, and if she associated Madame Antoine Charles with herself, she gave no sign. They walked down the steps towards the car and his hand was beneath her elbow, just as powerful, just as dominating as Madame's had been on the ascent. At the foot of the slope the car was waiting for them, the chauffeur stood holding the door open and Kate climbed inside.

Only when the vehicle began to pull smoothly away from the kerb was she able to shake herself from the sense of bewildered shock that had lain upon her since that moment in the vestry of the church. She turned to the man by her side, asking in a distracted tone beyond which there was a hint of wildness, 'What's happened?' Her voice broke in a sob. 'Where is Antoine?'

'Hush! One moment.' His English was as fluent as Antoine's and his voice was similar, but deeper, with a disturbing mellow quality. Kate watched him lean forward to press a button which caused the glass panel to slide closed between the driver and themselves, and only then did he turn to look full at her, his face not showing anything of what he might be feeling.

That was when Kate realised for the first time just how closely he resembled Antoine. Indeed, he might almost have been him, except that his face was a little leaner, the features more hawklike, harder somehow, the eyes, although dark like Antoine's, were slightly slanting as if some Oriental gene had crept into his inheritance. And they were fierce with none of the melting tenderness she remembered. He was taller too; dully she remembered that even with the smothering veil she had known that. But now the dark eyes were assessing her as closely as she was him, the strongly

marked eyebrows came together in an appraising way
and the narrow lips smiled showing teeth that gleamed
whitely against the dark skin.

'And what are you thinking, Kate?' There was a hint
of amusement in his voice, but whether she or he himself was the source of that amusement she could not
discern. 'Are you thinking that indeed I might be
Antoine?'

'No.' Not that. Never that, she thought. Her heart
was palpitating beneath the thin material of her dress.
She was conscious of its violence but unaware that her
face was as parchment-white as the wedding gown itself. With what strength she could summon she spoke
as firmly as she could. 'Please, would you explain this
fiasco? And tell me, please,' she was unable to keep the
note of appeal from her voice, 'please tell me what's
happened to Antoine!'

'Will you trust me?' One slightly sinister eyebrow
shot up enquiringly. 'Trust me to explain everything
later?'

'Trust you?' Not very successfully she tried to inject
into the words the scorn she felt for him. Instead in her
voice she heard wildness and hysteria. 'Why should I
trust you?' She caught her lower lip between her teeth.

'Because I fear,' and his face now had grown sombre,
the dark penetrating eyes surveyed her fiercely, 'I very
much fear that there is no one else you *can* trust.'

'I shall tell the very first person that I meet that
you're not the man I meant to marry!'

He laughed briefly. 'Then why did you not say so in
church? You allowed me to kiss you in there, you
walked out on my arm. Do you think it would be credible to make such a statement now? What would the

guests think?' He was blatantly mocking now. 'Merely that the bride was showing maidenly reticence such as is seldom seen these days. That the bride needed her mother's reassurance and that it was a pity she was alone. But they would trust that the bridegroom's gentleness would make her forget such understandable female vapourings.'

'I hate you!' Impulsively Kate raised her fists and beat him on the chest, but at once her hands were captured in one of his and held against the gleaming white shirt. 'I hate you!' she repeated, but now was conscious of his heart beating strongly beneath her fingers and the comforting warmth of his clasp. Her sobs died away, and at last he released her and took a handkerchief from his pocket to wipe her cheeks.

'Forgive me, *ma petite*.' Now there was so much tenderness that she had to cast a quick glance at him simply to confirm that indeed he was not Antoine. 'Forgive me for being unkind to you. Especially when I promised Antoine that I would be especially tender towards you, his darling Kate.'

'Antoine?' It was a mere whisper as the violet eyes searched his face.

'*Oui*—Antoine is my cousin. And for his sake I agreed to this foolish escapade.'

'Antoine *asked* you to do this . . .?'

'Yes.'

'I don't believe you!' She turned away from him, staring through the glass at the passing countryside without seeing it, hardly aware when they swept past the wide gates, past the stone greyhounds as uncaring as she, along towards the sweeping front entrance of the château.

'Well, what is it to be?' His voice was warm and persuasive, tempting her gaze from the pale gravel of the
drive back to his face. 'Will you trust me?' he asked
after a pause.

'No. No!' In an effort to harden her resolve she
shook her head desperately. 'Of course I shan't trust
you. Damn you!' She spat the words at him, scarcely
noticed the way his mouth tightened. 'Where is
Antoine? Why should he ask you to look after me
when all he wants is to marry me himself?' She had
raised her fists for another attack on the immaculate
darkness of his suit when the car glided to a halt.

'Be quiet!' The cold whip of his words made her
hesitate and his eyes as he looked down at her were as
dark as mountain tarns. 'Be quiet, I tell you.' The
hands that caught hers were cruel and ruthless. 'If you
wish to help Antoine, then you must do as I say. That
is better.' With a contemptuous little gesture he thrust
her hands away from him. 'And now be careful.
Gérard!' He made a warning movement towards the
chauffeur who was coming round to open the door for
them. 'Everything will be reported to *Madame ma tante*
later. Let us give her no more satisfaction than we can
help.'

'Help Antoine?' That was almost the only phrase
that had lodged itself into Kate's troubled thoughts.
'What do you mean? Is he in danger?'

'No, of course he is not.' He smiled down at her with
a bewildering change of manner. 'He is perfectly fit and
well.' The car door opened and he raised one of her
hands to his mouth. 'I cannot explain now. But I can
only tell you that with me you are safe. Let us get this
farce of a wedding over as soon as possible, and then I

shall tell you everything. Simply trust me.'

And incredibly, that was what she did. Afterwards she could never explain why. Was it merely that there was no one else in that château whom she could trust? Certainly not Madame! And Bernice? All along she must have known what was going to happen. Or was Kate's decision to trust this tall dominating man an instinctive response to an overwhelming personality? Whatever the reason, only the fact that he was by her side kept her going through that dreamlike ritual.

It might have been rather charming with the right man, she thought dully. One long table, elegantly perfect with snowy damask and gleaming crystal, accommodated the twenty guests who had come from the church to the wedding breakfast. Vaguely Kate recognised the two couples who had dined with them last night, but she knew none of the others present. Madame, who had arranged the delicious meal, smiled and nodded as she was complimented, but her eyes hardly ever left Kate's face and the triumph in them penetrated even into the girl's distracted thoughts.

If the guests thought that the bride was singularly quiet and that she showed little interest in the food then no doubt it was considered only natural, especially in a bride so young, 'si ravissante', and so unlucky to be without her mother on this special day in her life. But on the other hand she was fortunate to have a husband so attentive as Monsieur Antoine Charles.

Kate sat and listened to the speech by the man whom she had just mistakenly married; vaguely she was aware that the guests were amused by what he was saying, and once or twice she noticed that one or two of the younger women glanced meaningfully from her to the bridegroom, perhaps with a hint of envy in their eyes. But most of the time she sat looking impassively in front of her as if none of what was happening concerned Kate Ellerdale.

Only once was she in danger of losing control of herself, and that was when Madame Savoney-Morlet, who was sitting laughing with her guests, allowed her contemptuous smile to linger over the bride's features.

'Perhaps it is time for you to go up to change, *mademoiselle*. Oh,' in mocking apology she put her hand to her lips, 'but of course it is no longer *mademoiselle*, it is *madame*.'

Kate felt the colour rise in her cheeks as anger swept like a torrent through her, but before she could spit out the angry words she felt a hand touch hers.

'It is time to change, *chérie*.' The words were as tender as any of the guests could have wished. She stared into his eyes for a moment, surprising in their depths something that might have been admiration, before she turned again to the woman opposite.

'Of course.' She was aware that Bernice had risen from her seat at the end of the table, that she was coming forward asking if the bride required any help.

'No, thank you, Bernice.' Summoning up all her energies, Kate was able to speak in a cool controlled voice. 'Only if you would please take the pins out of the headdress.' She waited for a moment until the securing pins had been handed to her. 'Thank you, Bernice.' With a vague smile at the assembled guests she walked over to the door behind her which led to a side staircase.

It was a capricious little breeze that caught her veil, pulling the coronet from her head as she passed a pink rose which climbed and tumbled against the wall. And in her hurry the fine material caught on a hundred piercing briars, tearing, and she pulled at it in a vain attempt to save it.

Behind her she heard an anguished cry from Madame Savoney-Morlet, who sprang from her seat and came hurrying over. Kate turned with well-disguised enquiry to a face distorted with fury as the woman tried to extricate the filmy material from the barbarous thorns. Her low voice was venomous in a way that transcended language barriers, and Kate, with a feeling of barren triumph, turned and walked swiftly upstairs to her bedroom.

Just for a moment she stood looking at herself in the long spotted glass, seeing the smooth lines of the dress matching the curves of her figure. Then her fingers were scrabbling for the zip, she was dragging it over her head, discarding all the fine underwear which had been such a blissful extravagance, replacing them with an old pair of jeans and a simple checked blouse.

When she had changed, she pushed the pretty cream suit she had intended wearing into one of her cases along with the defiled wedding-dress, unaware that the sound of her sobbing breaths echoed through the room and along the corridor. She was pressing down the lid when she heard the door open and without turning round she knew that Madame was standing there, watching. The strength of the older woman's feelings was so compulsive that Kate had to force herself to continue what she was doing.

'You realise . . .' the grating tones of the voice arrested Kate's hand as she struggled with the lock of her case, '. . . you have ruined something quite irreplaceable with your carelessness.'

'Ruined? What?' Kate looked up as if genuinely puzzled, only the whiteness of her knuckles as her fingers closed round the handle of the suitcase betraying her emotion. Her eyes moved to the cloud of veiling in the woman's hands. 'Oh, you mean that old veil.' She busied herself with the keys, but her tension showed when next she spoke. 'But it served its purpose, did it not, *madame*? To hide the truth from me.' Her voice shook, but she struggled with the words. 'What have you done, *madame*? To me, to Antoine?'

Madame's laugh, unpleasant and with a hint of wildness, brought Kate's eyes up to look into the slightly deranged brilliant eyes. 'As to you, *mademoiselle*, I do not give that.' There was a world of contempt in the viciously snapped fingers. 'But Antoine—*mon fils*.' Her voice softened. '*Mon cher fils*. My poor foolish boy! For him,' a smile played about the red carmined mouth, 'for my child I would risk everything, to protect him from himself.'

There was something so unattractive about the strange mixture of venom and weakness on the woman's face that Kate experienced a frisson of horror at the base of her spine.

'But why, *madame*?' She forced the words through lips that were stiff as panic threatened to overwhelm her. 'Why? Forcing me to go through that awful, awful . . .' She bit her lip furiously, then searched the face opposite her, that cold dark face with the frightening gleaming eyes, for some clue, some explanation of what had happened. 'Where is Antoine? Is he ill? Has something . . .'

'Antoine is perfectly well. He has come to his senses

in time, that is all.' There was no mistaking the sneering satisfaction on the other woman's face. 'Did you think that a girl like you, little better than a shop-girl, could be allowed to marry the owner of the Savoney-Morlet estates? Our family is one of the most ancient in France and for three centuries there has been no foreign blood in our veins. Do you think that I would ever allow my son to be the one who committed such folly?' She laughed with careful scorn. 'How could you presume? You, who have no understanding of us, *une anglaise*! I am surprised at your foolish impertinence.' Her theatrical intensity was chilling.

'Then why didn't you simply tell me?' At last Kate's fragile self-control collapsed and there was no halting the tears that welled from her eyes and streamed down her cheeks. 'Why didn't someone tell me? Why didn't Antoine tell me?' She fought against rising hysteria. 'Why go through all this show, all this sordid pretence of marriage?'

There was a long silence while the coal black eyes glittered in genuine amusement. 'Antoine. *Cher* Antoine,' she spoke slowly as if savouring the words, 'he has always been so kind-hearted. I've no doubt that he saw how it was with you and wished not to disappoint. When he reached home he realised how inappropriate such an alliance would be, he changed his mind, but could not bring himself to admit it to you. And he was content to allow his mother to arrange things for him. But as to that other matter, *mademoiselle*,' she used the word with deliberate malice and offence, 'the one you called pretence—there was no pretence, of course. There is not the faintest doubt that you are legally married to my nephew Antoine Charles,' suddenly she snapped her fingers again in a last gesture of demonic triumph, 'and I wish you joy of each other!' A mad look blazed eerily in the hooded eyes as she closed the door behind her.

In spite of the anguish tearing at her, Kate felt as they drove through the high stone gates of the château a faint lightening of her spirits, as if she were leaving some malign influence. She lay back in her seat, her mind utterly empty, exhausted from the emotional strain, weary of attempting to understand or even to consider what had happened to her that day.

And when she felt the car slide to a stop by the roadside the eyes she turned to the man she had just married were cloudy with bewilderment. She felt his finger touch her cheek, saw his lips move. Antoine's lips and eyes—and yet not. His voice—and yet . . .

'Kate.' Flaring eyebrows were drawn together in a frown of concern. 'You are suffering from shock. And who can be surprised, *ma petite*? A stay at the château must be that and more, much more for someone unprepared. And I suspect,' the dark eyes searched her features with an intensity that scored her, 'I suspect that Antoine gave you no preparation?'

The gentleness of his tone brought the pain achingly back to her chest and she shook her head, unable to speak. His touch brushed the tumbled hair back from her cheek. 'Will you trust me? I'm asking you again.' A faint smile lingered about his mouth.

'Trust you?' She spoke without understanding.

'Yes. Look, *chérie*,' he reached into the rear seat and brought out a basket, 'you ate nothing at the wedding breakfast and I suppose at *petit déjeuner* you were too excited to have anything, so I'm going to insist that you have some food now.' Lifting the lid of the basket, he took two glasses which he balanced on the open flap of the glove compartment. Kate saw the lean brown fingers strip some gold foil from the top of a small bottle and begin to ease out the stopper. When the glasses were filled with the sparkling liquid he handed one to her.

'Drink,' he commanded, and to make certain he held her lifeless fingers round the slender stem before reaching out for his own glass. 'To you.' His face was very serious. 'To you, my beautiful Kate.'

Unexpectedly, for no reason, her eyes flooded with tears, but she turned quickly away, hoping that he hadn't noticed.

'Drink, Kate.' Grateful that he made no remark about the tears, she raised the glass to her mouth and gulped, surprised and thankful when it surged fierily through her veins, seeming actually to disperse that other ache. And almost without noticing she put out her other hand to take from him the tiny pieces of bread, buttered and liberally spread with pâté, as they were handed to her.

'That's better.' He took the empty glass from her and wiped her mouth with the napkin he had spread over her knee, responding to the almost imperceptible twitch of her lips with a laugh. 'Now I'm going to suggest that you go to sleep, *chérie*.' He got out of the car and going round to the passenger door he pulled her out and to her feet. For a moment, affected by the wine, she swayed towards him so that his hands came out to steady her, linking easily round her waist while the dark eyes looked down at her, no longer gentle, but rather cold, appraising.

'I'm sorry.' Kate blushed and put up an unsteady hand to brush the hair back from her face.

His eyes skimmed over her again before he released her and bending down inside the car he adjusted her seat so that it was transformed into a bed. He tossed down a cushion for a pillow, then turned to help her inside. Obediently she got in, grateful to be able to lay her head down, to try to seek a few hours' oblivion from the nightmare that life had so suddenly become

She heard his door slam, felt the soft touch of a mohair rug as it was spread over her, the brief impersonal touch of his hand as he spoke.

'Go to sleep, Kate. We have a long drive ahead of us. When we come to the end of our journey then you can have all of your questions answered.' He seemed to wait for a reply, but when none came Kate heard a faint sigh.

Then the engine fired and she felt the smooth swift acceleration of the vehicle as they spun away from the quiet roadside parking place. Kate lay with her eyes firmly closed, and as she succumbed to the mesmeric swish of the tyres on the dry roads she knew that sleep and healing oblivion were stealing over her. Despair ebbed away. Her breathing became deep and regular and she slept.

Darkness had almost fallen when she became aware of hands none too gently trying to shake her into wakefulness, while some deep instinct told her to keep her eyes closed to feign sleep, to avoid returning to a life where pain lurked so unexpectedly. But the man who was speaking her name so urgently would have none of her evasion and slapped her cheek gently, letting her know that his patience was not endless.

'Come on, Kate! I know you're awake now.'

'No.' She thrust his hands away and turned to bury her face in the pillow. 'No!'

'But yes.' He grasped her hands and in one swift sure movement pulled her to her feet.

Kate looked at him for a moment before she remembered everything that had happened, then her eyes flashed in sudden anger. 'You!' She spat the word at him, making it sound like an insult.

To her annoyance her show of temper appeared only to amuse him, for he grinned at her. 'But yes. I have not been transformed into anyone more acceptable while you slept. Alas, I am your companion. And,' his voice hardened, his smile faded abruptly, 'and alas, you are mine. Shall we make the best of it?'

'I didn't choose you!' she flared back. 'I had nothing to do with the situation we're now in.' It angered her to think that he was the first man who had ever expressed disappointment at being with her.

'That is true, Kate. And I apologise for my lack of gallantry. Shall we just say that for the moment we are stuck with each other and . . .'

'Is that supposed to be an apology?'

'That we are stuck with each other and should try to make the best of things. And I am tired after driving so long. And hungry. If I fall short of your expectations then perhaps you will remember that and excuse me. But now, shall we go inside? I'm sure that after a meal we shall both feel better. And I can positively guarantee that the cooking at La Chaumière will please you.'

For the first time Kate looked around her, seeing that they were in the parking place of a small restaurant.

From the small square windows soft light spilled invitingly and through the screen of trees she could see tables set out on a terrace, heard the murmur of voices, the clink of glasses and cutlery. And mingling with the scents of the countryside she could discern mouth-watering smells of roasting meat, the delicious aroma of freshly roasted coffee, and she realised that what he said was only too true. She was starving and if she didn't eat soon she would faint from sheer hunger.

Without waiting for her assent he put one hand on her elbow and guided her firmly in the direction of the door of the hotel. She found herself in the tiny foyer and hung back while her companion went forward to the desk where a man was absorbed in some account books.

'*Bon soir*, Henri.' That much Kate recognised, but the rest of the conversation was much too rapid and voluble to mean anything. Only the pleasure of the proprietor when he looked up and recognised his client needed no explanation. They continued to talk for some time and Kate turned away from the man's searching interested eyes as he looked from her to the book that lay open on the desk in front of him. She stood gazing into a glass display case on the wall beside the door studying the array of local fossils with a quite misleading appearance of interest, but seeing in the reflection that the proprietor turned to fidget with the keys which were hanging on numbered hooks.

But before she had time to reflect on the significance of that they were both standing beside her and she was being introduced, the owner of the hotel was holding her hand, bowing over it and was clearly offering his congratulations. Dismayed blue eyes sought the dark ones which responded with mocking amusement before, seeming to take pity on her at last, he came forward and touched her arm again.

'Henri is a little surprised to know that I am married, but he says now that he has seen you he quite understands.' The fingers round her arm tightened warningly. 'It is a compliment to you.'

'Oh . . .' It was an effort to force her stiff lips into a smile, as she tried to make some response. '*Merci, monsieur.*'

Henri smiled again, bowed, then turned in the direction of the restaurant, showed them to a seat in a corner, then with another murmur of congratulations to Kate, he picked up two large handwritten menus and handed one to each of them.

'*Eh bien*, Monsieur Charles.' And he was gone.

Kate stared at the long list of incomprehensible dishes without understanding a word of them and at last laid it down. 'At least now I know you have a name.'

The dark eyes opposite flicked up at her for a moment before returning to the menu. 'You doubted it?'

'You never told me what it was.'

'But I thought you knew, my dear,' he drawled. 'My aunt used it often enough. The priest used it in our marriage service. It is Antoine Charles Savoney-Morlet—almost but not quite the one you expected to have.'

'I could never call you Antoine!' she burst out passionately, ignoring the waiter who was hovering, pad and pencil at the ready, beside their table.

'Then,' his tightened lips, the coldness of his eyes were warning her, 'it is as well there is no need. I have always been called Charles. I prefer it.' Dismissing her, he turned to signal the waiter and together the two men pored over the menu, leaving Kate to smoulder with angry frustration. There were only about eight tables in the room, but through the open doors other diners could be glimpsed on the terrace which she had noticed earlier. Inside it seemed an unpretentious little place with checked covers on the tables and matching red and white shades on the lamps. But the customers looked a fairly prosperous lot. Kate noticed that the women were all dressed up, with immaculate make-up and hair. Nervously she put up a hand to her own tumbled head, pushed her blouse down firmly inside her jeans and wished she had gone to the ladies' room before coming inside. At the very next table sat a woman dressed as if she were going to Glyndebourne, in soft pastel chiffon, and round her neck a slender silver chain with a dark red stone hanging against her smoothly powdered skin.

As if aware that she was being studied, the woman suddenly looked up at Kate, the interested stare appearing to take in every detail of her slightly dishevelled appearance before moving on to Charles, who seemed an infinitely more intriguing spectacle. Then she leaned forward and without taking her eyes off Charles, murmured a few words to her companion. At once, with total lack of discretion, the man turned round in his seat, his eyes first encountering Kate's discouraging stare and then moving on swiftly. It took him just a moment to make up his mind, apparently, for he returned to his wife and gave a confirmatory nod. Again the woman looked at Kate, questioningly, disbelievingly, before returning again to Charles, who was still engaged with the waiter.

At last their discussion came to an end, the waiter completed his scribbling, nodded once or twice as a final word was spoken, picked up the two menus which he held under one arm and moved away, threading his way between the tables towards the door which Kate had decided led to the kitchen.

'Do you know the people at the next table?' Kate sounded aggressive, which was she decided as good a way as any of keeping the nightmares at bay.

Charles looked coolly at her for a moment before turning in the direction she had indicated with an abrupt little movement of her hand. 'Do you mean the attractive woman in the saffron-coloured dress and the man in the pale grey suit?'

'Yes.' Without looking round at them she was able to confirm what they were wearing.

'No, I don't think so.' He paused. 'Why do you ask?'

'They appeared to be talking about us . . . about you,' she amended quickly.

He shrugged as if the matter held no interest for him. Then, 'I ordered for you as you appeared to have no interest in deciding for yourself. I hope you have no great likes and dislikes.'

'I'm not interested in thinking about food at the moment,' she said not quite truthfully.

'Ah well,' there was that faint annoying smile on his mouth again, 'then we should have no difficulty. I ordered for you snails to start, then squid cooked in ink and for the main course, I was sure you would be sorry to miss the area's speciality, day-old foal cooked with herbs in red wine.'

Kate failed to notice the gleam in his eye and stared

at him in dismay. 'But,' her voice was faint with dis-belief, 'I can't possibly eat that! You had no right to order such things without asking me!'

'But you showed no interest. And I simply wanted you to have a meal that you will remember.'

'But I can't . . .'

'You can. You must.' He glanced up and nodded at the man who was offering a bottle of wine for inspection, then waited while their glasses were filled with the golden sparkling liquid. 'You must, my dear Kate. If you do not eat his food Henri will be so insulted. Besides, you must try strange dishes before you know whether or not you will like them.' He raised his glass and looked deeply, intensely into her eyes. 'To you, Kate.'

Without thinking she raised the glass and sipped, then sat back as the waiter appeared and put in front of each of them a small Ogen melon, wished them '*bon appetit*' and withdrew. Kate looked at her plate, across at his, then into his face, for the first time recognising that gleam in his eyes for what it was.

'You didn't mention melon.' Gravely she removed the serrated top and picked up her spoon.

'No, the melon I forgot. This is quite innocuous, Kate—chilled melon with port.' Suddenly he laughed aloud and covered her hand which was lying on the cloth with one of his. 'Forgive me for teasing you, Kate.'

To her annoyance she smiled. She hadn't meant to soften towards him, but there was something infectious about his amusement, something she couldn't resist. And perhaps the knowledge that the beautiful woman at the next table had looked across at him, her eyes going towards their linked hands, had some effect on her. Or maybe it was just her natural response to a handsome man. Whatever it was she smiled and was rewarded by a softening of his expression, a faint comforting pressure of his hand before he released it.

'Now,' his tone was almost caressing, 'I can understand why . . .'

She interrupted him before he could say the words that would make her think. 'I feel so conspicuous.' She shrugged and lifted up the long-handled spoon. 'Dressed in jeans and a blouse when everyone else is done up to the nines.'

His laugh made a tiny tingle run down the length of her spine so that she looked at him in dismay. 'Yes, Kate. But you must know that even in those, even with your hair uncombed, you're enough to make most men look twice. You know,' he leaned forward so that the woman who was looking at them must have thought they were discussing some intimate matter, 'when you came down today wearing that outfit, seeing the look on my aunt's face almost made the whole thing worth while. Such a disgrace, a Savoney-Morlet having so little *savoir faire*—even an Antoine Charles Savoney-Morlet. It will be a long time before she forgives the slur on the family honour.'

'You speak,' as she spoke she raised a piece of the delectably ripe melon to her mouth. 'You speak as if you dislike your aunt.' She waited, her head held interrogatively to one side, until he looked up, his eyes searching hers closely.

'Does that surprise you?' Then when she didn't answer he persisted. 'You found her so easy to like?'

'No.' Kate looked down, wondering why she found

the thought of melon so distasteful. 'I think I've never met a woman whom I dislike more. I can't,' her voice trembled, 'I can't believe that she's Antoine's mother.'

'Well, assuredly she is. And perhaps it is because she is the woman she is that she has made her son into the man he is.'

'How dare you!' She hissed the words at him, not noticing the interested glance from the next table. 'I shan't listen to a word against him! He's the best and kindest . . .'

'Hush, child!' Charles paused in the act of taking a spoonful of melon to his mouth and smiled tolerantly at her. 'You have no need to convince me of his virtues. I swear.' His face became so serious that she had no cause to doubt him. 'I swear that I love him as much as you do. What I said is quite simply the truth. And I think you will have little reason for denying the baleful influence she has upon him. No one more.' The dark eyes continued to bore steadily into hers. 'Now come on, eat your melon. The snails will be along soon.' He grinned at her. 'And let me fill your glass, it would be a pity to allow this champagne to spoil.'

'You ought not to have been so extravagant.' Almost unwillingly her hand went out, taking the glass to her mouth again. 'I thought champagne was only for celebrations. What have we to celebrate?'

'Our marriage.' His mocking voice taunted her. 'In spite of everything we were married today. Although,' he put down his glass and leaned back in his chair, 'no one would take you for a bride—more like a student on a hitch-hiking tour of France.' He leaned forward, lowering his voice so that they could speak more intimately. 'Do you think the elegant lady at the next table is thinking such a thing? That I have given you a lift and now I am trying to persuade you to . . .' He smiled as he watched the colour come up under her skin, but turned round when the waiter arrived to clear their plates and then put plates of small grilled trout in front of them.

'I cancelled the snails.' He smiled at her. 'I hope you will like that.'

And Kate thought that she had never tasted quite such delicious fish, cooked in butter with just a flavouring of garlic. And when she had the next course, which turned out to be escalope of veal with green salad, she decided that Charles's claims about the cooking in La Chaumière had not been exaggerated.

'Now,' Charles sat smiling at her as she chased the last sliver of meat round her plate, 'you will have some cheese?'

'No.' Kate sat back with a sigh. 'That was the most marvellous meal and I couldn't eat another thing.'

'No?' The wicked eyebrow arched in disbelief. 'But you must try one of Henri's desserts. He would be offended if you were to refuse. I can recommend the bavarois.'

Kate tried not to be tempted. In spite of everything the words Beverley Ann had spoken that day came back into her mind to taunt her. But still, she had always had a very sweet tooth and there was no denying that the way he had allowed the word to roll round his tongue made it sound irresistible. She tried to ignore the little warning voice telling her she had had too much to drink, that she wasn't used to champagne with her meals. She tried all those things and failed miserably.

'All right.' Her eyes gleamed in amusement. 'I shall

do as you say and try the bavarois.'

'Good girl!' His eyes commended her. Then, still smiling at her, he summoned the waiter and ordered cheese for himself and the pudding for her.

His amusement continued as he watched her clean her plate, the tip of her tongue coming out to lick the last spot of vanilla cream from her lips. Then after seeking her permission he leaned back in his chair and lit a long thin cheroot, the dark eyes surveying her with a curiosity that made her cheeks burn, caused her fingers to fidget restlessly with the stem of her glass.

'We shall spend the night here.' He hunched over the table to stir his coffee, no longer looking across the table at her but down into the dark depths of the whirling steaming liquid.

'Oh?' Suddenly her heart was thudding against her chest. She was looking at him with the great violet eyes, urging him to look at her, to explain what he meant. But he did not, and Kate was all at once aware of the pain in her head, remembered too late that she had no head for alcohol and that in the morning she would regret . . . everything. She emptied her cup in one gulp and watched him do the same before he pushed back his chair. It screeched loudly over the bare floor, but as everyone else seemed to have disappeared it didn't matter.

'Which case do you want me to bring up?' In the foyer he turned to her, his expression distant now, impenetrable.

'The small one has my things in it.' Was that thin childish voice really her own?

'I'll ask Henri to show you up.' He strode away from her and caught the proprietor just as he came through from the back. She heard them exchange words about the room and a moment later she was following the man up a narrow stair, answering his incomprehensible conversation with meaningless agreement.

In spite of her heightened emotions she was surprised and pleased by the room into which she was shown, for it was large and airy and in the open windows white net curtains moved in the warm night air. The walls were covered with a pretty paper with a pink and green pattern of roses and the wide bed had a pink candlewick cover thrown over it. Quickly Kate averted her eyes from that and followed the direction of Henri, who threw open what she had imagined was a cupboard door to reveal a small bathroom.

'*Merci*, Monsieur Henri.' She had no idea how she was able to speak so naturally, but when the door closed quietly behind him she had the urge to run downstairs after him and throw herself sobbing on to his shoulder. But before she had the chance to do so there was a brief tap at the door and Charles came in carrying her case, and a small one which presumably belonged to him.

'Hmm.' Appraisingly he glanced round. Then he put the cases down and went over and stuck his head inside the bathroom door. Kate lowered herself on to the edge of the bed and only just stopped her hands going to the neck of her blouse in a protective gesture that would undoubtedly have made him laugh. 'Is this adequate for you?' He was standing looking down at her now, his keen eyes doubtless seeing the way the colour was coming and going in her cheeks.

'Of course.' She tried to speak casually, as if she was in the habit of finding herself alone in bedrooms with strange men, and by chance married to one of them.

'*Bon.*' He bent down with unflattering relief and picked up his case from where he had placed it on the floor. 'Then sleep well, *ma petite.*'

'You . . . you're not staying here?' The words slipped out before she could stop them, regretting them immediately he swung round with that cold suspicious look on his face.

'You want me to?'

'Of course not.' If she had been less angry the tears would have come into her eyes and she would have hated him to see them.

Slowly he put down his case and sauntered back to her. 'No?' The eyes searched clinically, then quite suddenly he laughed. 'No, of course you do not. And that is just as well, my Kate, for I am determined that when Antoine comes to take possession of his bride he will find her . . . intact.' As she stared up at the mesmeric eyes Kate wondered if he could hear her heart pounding. Perhaps he might even be able to see it through the thin material of her blouse.

'At least,' as he turned back to the door it seemed that he spoke the final words with reluctance, 'as far as I'm concerned.' The closing of the door almost drowned his words, but she knew she had heard correctly.

CHAPTER THREE

KATE had no idea when she began to have those awful feelings about Charles. Surely it couldn't have been that first day, that very first day when she went downstairs and found him sitting in the bar of La Chaumière apparently involved in the news he was reading from the paper which he held up in front of him. She stood for a moment in the shadows watching, seeing the dark brows drawn together in concentration as his eyes skimmed over the printed pages, noting how the sunlight slanting through the windows illuminated one side of his face and leaving the other in shadow, the hairs on the backs of the long dark fingers gleaming almost golden in the light.

Perhaps she moved and attracted his attention, perhaps some sixth sense warned him, for when she looked at his face again she saw that his eyes were on her. At once he folded his paper and rose, coming forward to meet her. In contrast to the dark suit he had worn for the whole day yesterday, he had changed into pale linen slacks and a checked shirt with a dark tie. His hair glistened damply as if he had just left the shower,

'Kate.' He put his hand on her arm, pulling her towards the plain wood table, waiting until she was seated before taking his place opposite her, leaning one elbow on the table and supporting his chin in his hand. 'You slept well?'

'Yes.' She coloured faintly and blinked back the unexpected tears. 'Does that seem awful?'

'Of course it does not. I'm glad.' For the first time he smiled at her. 'And now you are dying for breakfast?'

'Not for breakfast. Just for coffee. Gallons and gallons of coffee.'

'Good.' He signed to the waiter who was sitting behind the bar reading a magazine. 'Sure you wouldn't prefer tea?'

'No, I drink coffee in the mornings. Although I don't expect to get instant when I'm in France.'

'That I can promise.' He spoke rapidly to the young man who returned to the bar and the gleaming chromium apparatus which began to steam and hiss as the coffee-making operation began its cycle. A few moments later he returned with paper napkins and bowls, setting them on the table with a basket of freshly baked rolls, a large pot of coffee and one of milk.

'Black, please.' The preference was stated before Kate had time to ask. 'Yes, in the bowls,' he added as she hesitated. Then when she had finished pouring, 'You haven't drunk from a bowl before?' He proceeded to show her how easy it was.

'No, never.' Following his example, she found that she had tilted the bowl too enthusiastically and that the hot liquid dribbled down her chin, on to her blouse. 'Well . . .' She dabbed not very effectively with the serviette.

'You'll learn.' The eyes that seemed to notice so much skimmed over her, making her aware that she was wearing the same drab jeans and blouse he had seen yesterday. She sensed and resented his disapproval. He pushed the basket of rolls towards her and returned to his newspaper.

Half an hour later they were driving along quiet roads, and to Kate's entranced eyes it seemed that France had been holding herself back, had been saving all her beauty for this special day. All the gloom and darkness of the last two days had disappeared and in their place were soft blue skies with here and there a patch of white woolly cloud, but even they were quickly chased by the sun's strengthening rays.

But even that didn't offer sufficient explanation for the entirely different feeling she had about the country they were driving through. For while she had positively disliked the scenery round Le Puy; this was nothing short of enchantment, a narrow curving road dotted with tiny charming villages which clung to the hillsides and everywhere was green, light, delicate, feathery and as fresh as if the leaves were newly burst from their buds. She said as much to Charles, looking up from the notes she was making on the piece of paper she had taken from her handbag.

'It's like fairyland, isn't it? So beautiful.'

'*I* think so.' Although he didn't take his eyes from the twisting road she sensed that her words had pleased. So she was pleased and was lingering thoughtfully upon the unexpected discovery of that pleasure when his next words began to paint another picture for her. 'You should see it in winter, when the snow lies thick on the mountains and roofs, when the trees droop under the weight of it on their branches. Then you would really know what fairyland looks like. This region is famous for its beauty, this Cantal.'

'The Cantal? Even the name is beautiful.'

'*Oui*. Les Monts du Cantal.' Then in a brisker tone, 'Do you ski, Kate?'

'Yes, a bit. I used to go up to Scotland to ski and we had a holiday once in Austria. For winter sports.'

'We?' There was a sharp querying note in the monosyllable.

'Hilary and I. She's the girl I shared a flat with at home.' The words had made her remember the warnings which she had chosen to ignore, and despite the sunshine and the dappled brightness she felt cold and shivered a little.

'Soon,' she had no idea if he had noticed her involuntary reaction, 'we shall stop and buy some food for a picnic. We have no need to hurry today.'

After that they sat for a long time without speaking. Kate felt afraid. Afraid of the time which must be fast approaching, the time when explanations could no longer be deferred, when she would have to ask him what they were doing together. When she might be obliged to hear those things which would be unbearable.

They were driving through Le Lioran when Charles pulled the car into the side of the road, switched off the engine and turning to her released her safety harness.

'Now,' he smiled, disturbingly near, 'I want you to go and buy first of all some bread. Then go to that *charcuterie* across the road and buy some *saucisson* for our picnic. Next door there's an *alimentation*, there you'll be able to get butter and some fresh cheese. Oh, and I see they have what look like some gorgeous peaches. Two of those. I shall follow you and pretend that I can't understand the language either. Afterwards I'll be able to tell you how you did.'

'But I can't!' Kate protested. 'And especially I can't if you're hovering in the background being critical. It would be like being back at school for an examination. One you know you're bound to fail.'

'All right. I shan't follow you. I'll go and get the *alimentation*. Here,' he pulled out a notecase and thrust a handful of money into her hand, 'you fetch the bread and sausage, I'll get the other things. Rendezvous here in ten minutes.'

Rather diffidently Kate went into the baker's shop, finding when she got inside and was presented with such a bewildering array of bread that even the few simple words needed for her purchase had deserted her. But within a few minutes she had made both the purchases, returning to the car a split second ahead of Charles, who came across laden with several paper bags and with a bottle of red wine under one arm.

'How did it go?' He turned to her when they had stowed their purchases away in the rear and just before he switched on the engine.

'Oh, no problem.' She heard the engine fire and turned to him with a laugh that caused him to raise an eyebrow in her direction.

'No problem?'

'None at all. For the rolls I simply pointed to what I wanted and held up four fingers. The girl appeared to understand perfectly.'

'And the *charcuterie*?'

'Oh, in there, it was a young man. I asked for *saucissons* and he said "How many, *mademoiselle*?" so there seemed no point in robbing him of the opportunity to speak English.'

They drove away from the small town until a few

miles farther on Charles swung the car off the road into what Kate at first thought was merely a parking area, but when she looked properly she saw that it was a huge picnic spot, beautifully clean with heavy wooden benches and tables sheltering under tall lime trees.

Charles produced the basket they had used the previous day and quickly rinsed the glasses under a tap which ran constantly into a huge stone trough and began to arrange the food at one of the tables.

'Sit down.' Before getting out of the car he had picked up sunglasses from the dashboard, so that now the expression in his eyes was even more difficult to discern. Kate decided to follow his example and pulled her own from her bag and perched them on her nose, sliding them into position with a long finger.

'That's better. Who would have thought there would be such a change in the weather after yester . . . day?' Her voice faded as she remembered that at this very time yesterday they had been standing close together in church, their hands touching, she thinking she was marrying Antoine. And he, what had he been thinking? Quickly she glanced at him, wondering if her words had meant anything to him, but he was polishing the glasses with a paper towel, taking a corkscrew from the basket. Suddenly she knew that she didn't want explanations. Not now. Not here. Nothing to spoil this perfect idyllic situation. Quickly her hands reached out for the small wax cartons of the meats and pâté she had bought in the *charcuterie*.

'I'm surprised . . .' her voice shook a little as she spoke, 'that there aren't more people here. I should have thought, at this time of year . . .' She looked about her at the few picnickers who were scattered about the vast area.

'Mmm.' Charles gave the impression of being slightly distracted as he filled the two glasses with deep red wine. 'Well,' he raised his glass towards her in a slightly morose gesture before drinking, 'if it had been a Sunday then we should have been unable to find a place. At weekends the whole population of the cities heads for the countryside and we should have found the area alive with dogs and children, grandmothers and cyclists. You see, they bring the children's bicycles in the back of the car and then they can have a Tour de France here in the picnic area.' He pushed the package of butter towards her with a knife. 'Would you begin, please, *chérie*. And butter some for me, if you will.'

'Of course.' Kate felt her fingers had grown clumsy and with him watching she found the rolls hard to split, the butter difficult to spread. Charles must have thought so too, for she found that he had taken the knife from her and was completing the small task with much more deftness than she had shown. Kate drank some of her wine, wondering mournfully if he was remembering yesterday and how he had fed her with tiny pieces of bread and pâté. She looked away from him into the valley, at all the changing colours of the treetops as the gentle breeze rippled through them. Hardly aware of what she was doing, she put out her hand for a piece of bread, then was astonished to realise how hungry she was.

They ate everything Kate had bought in the shop, then Charles produced two perfect large peaches from the bag and laughed as she bit into hers so that the juice ran down her skin and on to her blouse.

'I think,' she dabbed at her blouse again with the

handkerchief he obligingly handed to her, 'I think I shall have to rummage in a case and try to find a clean blouse.'

He didn't answer but continued to look at her with a faint smile before turning away and getting up to cross towards the car. She watched him, curiously dispassionate about that easy graceful stride, seeing the hair riffle and fall forward over his forehead as he bent to reach inside the car.

A moment later he was straightening up, his head turned to her but his eyes hidden by the smoked glass. Between his teeth he held a thin cheroot, a match flared as he lit it and stood breathing in the scented blue smoke with an air of satisfaction. Then he came across to the bench, and now she could see that his eyes were seeking hers, there was an air of determination about him that made her shiver slightly in spite of the sun's warmth.

But when he sat down he did not speak immediately, but his stare was so cool and persistent that Kate grew confused, her hands reached out for the debris of their lunch which she began to collect into one of the empty paper bags.

'Leave that for the moment.' His tone brooked no refusal and with uncharacteristic obedience she stopped, her troubled gaze fastened on the distant skyline. Her heart was thumping uncomfortably, but she could think of nothing to say. And his next words seemed to touch directly what she was feeling.

'You have no questions for me, Kate?' His voice was gentler than it had been before, yet almost more difficult to cope with. Miserably and still without looking at him she shook her head, then was perversely annoyed when she heard his low deep laugh. At once a deep flush coloured her skin, the eyes she turned on him were stormy with dislike.

'How dare you laugh!' Even as she flew at him she noticed that there was no amusement on his face. In fact it looked as cold and bleak as she felt. 'When *you've* put me in this horrible position!' Only the anger she felt stopped the tears that ached behind her eyes.

'I have put you in it?' Now there was a threat of danger in the very silkiness of his tone. 'Only I? Was there no one else who was at least partially to blame?'

'Oh, you mean Antoine, don't you?' At once she was on the defensive. 'But there must be some proper explanation. *He* wouldn't have chosen to make me endure all this.'

'Whereas I would.' She could see that his eyes had narrowed slightly. 'Is that what you mean, *ma chère*?'

'And don't call me that!' she snapped. 'It's so insincere. When you think that yesterday at this time we'd scarcely even met!'

'But you are my wife, Kate.' His lips were a thin hard line now, the dark eyebrows drawn together in a frown. 'And whatever you may think, this situation has meant a considerable sacrifice for me. You will have to be introduced to my friends and then later I shall have to explain that you prefer my young cousin Antoine. I shan't enjoy that, Kate.' He spoke the last words mildly, studied the glowing end of the cigar, then extinguished it on the sandy ground with a savage movement of his feet.

Kate sat staring at him, the enormity of the position dawning on her for the first time. She had been so immersed in her own misery and shock that she had not for a moment considered his. 'I . . . I . . . But . . .' she stammered. Then on a sob, 'Why?'

There was a long silence before he repeated her query with almost as much bewilderment as she had shown. 'Why, Kate? Why indeed? I have been asking the same question too since yesterday. All I can say is that for Antoine I have always been prepared to do most things, to set things right when he got them wrong. And he was so upset, so very persuasive on the telephone.'

'But why . . .?' The word was a whisper.

'Why? Because he cannot stand up to his mother. She has dominated him all his life—and before Antoine, his father and her stepdaughter. You see, Kate, the story goes back a long way. Our fathers, Antoine's and mine, were identical twins, and mine was the younger by about half an hour. They grew up inseparable even to the extent that they married cousins, Bernice's mother and mine. My mother died when I was three and Tante Jeanne when I was eight. In those days both families lived in the château, and it was understood that the estate would be shared between the two brothers who were so close in every way.

'But then my uncle remarried and everything changed. Although I was still too young to have the thing explained to me at that time I knew that there was some terrible tension in the house and the family solicitor appeared to spend all his time with us. I realised that it was involved with the new little cousin who had arrived, but I didn't understand in what way.

'Of course now it is clear enough that my uncle's second wife was very ambitious for her own child and wished to see me excluded. If my father had not died

suddenly from a heart attack things might have been
sorted out, but . . .' he shrugged, his face hard and
impassive, 'as it was the field was left clear for whatever
plans she wished to make. And of course they did not
include me. Only when I reached the age of twenty-one
did I learn that what I had thought of as my inheritance didn't belong to me at all. It was all Antoine's.
My uncle had died the previous year, and although
he always treated me kindly, there's no doubt that he
allowed himself to be dominated by his wife. As he
allowed his daughter, his whole household to be
dominated.'

'I'm sorry, Charles.' Helplessly she looked at him.
'But don't you resent it? I mean, that Antoine is . . .'

'I used to.' His smile was brief and bitter. 'Oh, not
that I blame Antoine—in fact I've always loved him.
He was the young brother I might have had if my
mother had lived. No, it wasn't his fault. His mother is,
as you know, a very . . . powerful woman, and he has
not the nature to stand up to her.'

'And so you were forced to leave your old home . . .'

'Not forced.' Again the cynical smile twisted his
mouth. '*Madame ma tante* kindly said that I could
always have a job on the estate. In other words she
invited me to go on running things. But only on the
understanding that I was the manager. Of course I
refused, and in spite of the various olive branches she
has held out I've kept myself apart from her pretty
much since then. I have felt freer since I escaped the
baleful influence of the château.'

'Until now . . .'

'*Oui.* As you say.' For the moment he appeared dis-
inclined to say any more.

'But I still can't understand.'

'Ah, forgive me. My mind was becoming involved
with old scores. The first I knew of you, my dear, was
when Antoine rang me to say that he had met you and
meant to marry you whatever his mother said. I was
delighted that at last he was standing up for himself and
told him to go ahead. Then a few days later I had
another message to say that his mother was pressing
him to be patient, and I could sense that he was weak-
ening, thinking that perhaps his mother was right. I
told him to stick to his original plans, for I've always
thought that a wife and family would be the best chance
he had of escape.' Suddenly, disarmingly, he grinned
at her. 'I don't know what it will do for you, Kate.
You'll have to be prepared to stand up for yourself.'

At the thought of it a sudden chill struck into her
bones and she shivered.

'Anyway, the next unexpected thing to happen was a
telephone call from Antoine's mother. She reminded
me that I had promised my uncle always to care for
Antoine and she thought that the time to put my promise into action had arrived. She has cool impudence,
hasn't she?' He looked at her, noting the paleness of her
face, then went on with his story.

'I was quite polite, so I'm sure she thought that I had
forgiven and forgotten, and when I had listened to her
story I laughed before asking her what she wanted me
to do. Surely, I said, you don't expect me to marry the
girl myself?

'There was a long pause and it suddenly occurred to
me that it was the sort of crazy thing that she might
even consider. And then later, when I sat down and
began to think about it, I saw the possibilities of the

position. Her fears would be completely assuaged and when the time came Antoine would come back and take you away.'

'But,' Kate's lips were stiff and she had to force the words from her lips, 'what reason did you give Antoine's mother? Surely she couldn't possibly imagine that you would do this thing simply to please her?'

'Ah no. Let us just say that I agreed to go ahead in her interests, for a consideration.'

Kate felt as if the life was being squeezed out of her body as he spoke the last words and as she was unable to look at him all her attention was concentrated on the small pile of paper on the table. 'And it doesn't seem to have occurred to either of you . . . Oh,' suddenly passionate she looked up at him, her eyes dark as midnight behind the smoked lenses, 'Oh, I'm not really blaming you. But Antoine is supposed to love me. How could he?'

'*Chérie!*' Reaching across the table, Charles took her chin in his hands, holding her head so that she had no chance of moving away from him. 'He does love you. I can think of no one for whom he would have risked so much. Be assured that when the time comes, he will come to me and demand that I return to him his wife.' A smile touched his mouth, more gentle than she had seen since he had begun the explanation. 'And then you and he will have the rest of your lives together. This will be simply an interval which you can tell your children about.' He released her then, coming round to stand beside her, he pulled her to her feet. 'And now we must be on our way.' He put out a hand and touched the stains on her blouse. 'You said that you wanted to change.' He seemed not to have seen the swift flush that his touch had brought nor the increased beat of her heart beneath the thin cotton. 'If you go and find what you want in your case, I'll tidy up here.'

Kate found a clean blouse in one of the large cases which had been stowed in the boot of his car and using the open door as a screen she slipped out of the soiled blouse and bent to pick up the fresh one from the seat just as Charles, his hands full of the remnants of their food, came round to stow them in the car. She was dressed in her jeans and a very brief revealing bra and saw his eyes rake her face, then her bare shoulders and swelling breast before turning abruptly from her. Kate's hands were shaking as she did up the buttons on the silky blue blouse.

'Ready?' His voice was impassive as he leaned inside the car, tossing his sunglasses casually on the dash-board as he did so.

'Yes.' Her manner was quiet, muted.

In the instant before he held the door for her their eyes met and she knew that he was thinking of that earlier moment, remembering her half-clad body. And the look in his eyes startled her. For Kate had been out with too many men who had wanted to make love to her to make any mistake about the signs.

But what from her point of view was infinitely more disturbing was her own reaction. For she longed to feel his mouth on hers—oh, not the brief formal em-brace she had experienced in church yesterday but something more searching and intimate, a kiss which she suspected would set her blood on fire. Of course it was all because he looked so much like Antoine. And she was feeling the frustration of her married yet unmarried situation. But she hoped, how she hoped, that the man she loved would not postpone their meeting for too long.

CHAPTER FOUR

LA PIGEONNIÈRE was not at all as she had expected it. For the rest of the afternoon as they drove at a leisurely pace along the valleys Charles had spoken easily, teasingly about the old pigeon loft he had bought when he had been forced to leave the château after his row with his aunt, how he had worked hard to convert it into a cottage which now had some of the comforts of modern living.

'How long ago was that, Charles?' asked Kate.

'That was ten—no, eleven years ago. You see, things are difficult when you suddenly find you have no money. I even had to find a career, some means of supporting myself.'

'And what did you do?'

'Oh, when I was unpacking my belongings I found a camera. I decided that perhaps I could keep the wolf from the door by taking family photographs and so on.'

'And did you?'

'What, did I take photographs? Or did I keep the wolf from the door?'

'Both.'

'Yes.' He laughed. 'I suppose I did.'

'And made enough to convert the pigeon shed?'

'Yes, for that too.'

'Good.' Although she said no more Kate decided

that he must have done fairly well, that was if his car and the obviously expensive clothes he wore were the result of his own efforts.

'Perhaps,' Charles spoke tentatively as if uncertain of her reaction, 'you will let me take your photograph. It might be the turning point in my career.' But there was a note in his voice that told her his suggestion was not entirely serious, that he was in some way testing her. She was considering how to reply when quite unexpectedly he swung the car off the narrow valley road, taking one which was even more restricted although just as beautiful with its overhead canopy of high lime trees.

'Look,' as they reached a gap in the trees one long dark finger pointed, 'La Pigeonnière. Home.' Kate noticed a small square tower peeping over the hill in the instant before they were swallowed again by the leafy tunnel. She slid round in her seat to steal a glance at the dark uncompromising profile, then was at once disturbed by the lightness of the expression that met hers.

'You sound relieved,' she said. Colour mounted in her cheeks and she stared forward through the windscreen. 'To be home, I mean.'

'I am.' He said no more, but Kate was conscious of an easing of the tension in him as they drove out of the trees, turned right along a wide gravel drive, through an arch in a high stone wall and stopped in a courtyard.

Only then did Kate understand how deceptive that first glimpse of the tower had been; that narrow square that edged over the hillside had betrayed little of the size and elegance of the property. The pigeon loft sat on top of a larger block, and buildings stretching out from it at right angles formed two sides of a courtyard. The third side was the wall with the archway which gave access to the road and the fourth was open to the descending hill.

The old stone of which the buildings were composed was the colour of dark honey, soft and warm so that even on the dullest day it would persuade one that somewhere the sun still shone. Kate swung her legs through the door which Charles held open for her, looking about her with eyes that made no attempt to hide her pleasure.

'This is what you call a pigeon loft?'

'Yes. And there they are, Kate.' Even before he answered she had heard the soft cooing, had felt her eyes drawn to the square tower where a few plump white doves stretched their wings and scratched lazily. One of them fluttered down to land on the paving stones by their feet, his tail fanning out behind him in a beautiful crescent as he pecked halfheartedly at the crevices in the hope of finding some food.

'Aren't they beautiful? It all is.' Kate walked away from Charles towards the open side, looking down into the valley far below where she could see the rich fields, the silver glint of water as it appeared and disappeared.

'That is the Vézère river. It joins the Dordogne not far from here.' He lingered with her, but it was her expression rather than the view which absorbed his attention. 'Now come inside, I want you to meet Madeau.' There was still a hint of tension about him as he took her arm and led her back to the front door where he had stopped the car.

'Madeau?' It was the first time she had heard the name and she looked at him in surprise.

'Yes. She lives with her husband in the flat over the garage.' He pointed to the large double doors in the adjoining wall and following his finger Kate could see light net curtains fluttering at the open windows on the second storey. 'Georges goes into Sarlat each day. He works in a garage and he does the garden in his spare time, Madeau looks after the house and does the cooking.'

As he spoke he led her up the few steps to the front door. It was set into the corner, recessed with heavy outer doors linked back on either side against the wall. Through the clear glass of the inner door set in a sur-round of rich mahogany Kate could see heavy old-fashioned wooden chests against plain white stone walls with many pieces of brass and copper catching the sunlight.

As he unlocked the door with the key Charles rang the doorbell, then ushered Kate in ahead of him. She had a moment to admire the clean simple lines of the large hall, the imposing sweep of the staircase in dark polished wood that branched out under a tall window and swept round to right and left.

'Madeau!' As he called her name and walked towards a closed door to the right of the hall, the door opened and a woman came through. She was younger than Kate had for some reason expected, about thirty-five, small and plump with rosy cheeks and her fair hair coiled up at the back of her head.

'Monsieur Charles!' Her face lit up at the sight of him, then she hesitated as she caught sight of Kate and she began to wipe her hands on the large white apron which enveloped her.

'This, Madeau,' Kate knew that he was anxious to

have the awkward moment over, 'this is my wife.'

For a moment there was a frown of incomprehension on the woman's face as she looked from her employer to the girl standing on the large Tabriz carpet which covered the floor. 'Your wife, Monsieur Charles?' The uncertainty of her manner told them that she was convinced she had misunderstood, and Kate felt herself grow warm with embarrassment.

'Yes, Madeau.' Charles laughed and came over to Kate and putting his arm round her drew her forward. 'I know it is a surprise to you, but this is my wife Kate. We were married only yesterday.'

'But, *monsieur*, such shocks!' The woman put her hand up to her mouth, pulling at her lip for a moment before she smiled and held out her hand to the newcomer. 'But such good shocks, *monsieur*. And *madame*.' All at once she seemed delighted with the situation and her grip on Kate's hand was warm and reassuring.

'Yes, and now you know why you spent that time with Madame Malvaud in London all those years ago. It was so you could learn English and make things easier for my wife when I found her.'

'Oh, *monsieur*!' Madeau smiled, obviously used to his teasing. 'But so sudden, *monsieur*. And so romantic, *madame*!'

'Thank you.' Kate felt a relaxation within herself and for the first time realised how great her own nervousness had been.

'Now, Madeau, would you take Madame Charles upstairs to the garden bedroom and I shall bring her cases.'

'*Mais certainement, monsieur. Madame, venez.*' Quickly removing her overall, rolling it up and putting it on a chair that stood at the foot of the stairs, Madeau turned indicating that Kate should follow. She paused at the small landing below the window to look out before continuing, her hands sliding smoothly over the polished banister.

'It's a beautiful house.' Kate tried to cover the awkwardness of the situation by the inconsequential remark. 'When Charles spoke of La Pigeonnière I had no idea it would be so large and so elegant.'

'Ah, Monsieur Charles . . .' Madeau shrugged as she led the way along the corridor and then paused before a closed door. 'He always jokes, *n'est-ce pas, madame?*'

'Yes,' Kate agreed without conviction, deciding that although her own view did not accord with Madeau's it was best to go along with it at the moment.

'*Et voilà, madame!*' With the air of producing a rabbit from a hat Madeau threw the door open, and when she saw it Kate could understand the woman's pride.

The room was fairly large and two high arched windows in the wall opposite the door made it light and airy, although the net curtains hanging across them sheltered the room from excessive heat in summer. One wall was lined with cupboards, all in a pale golden wood which complemented the period of the house and the other wall, indeed the whole room was dominated by the bed which stood against it. It had four slender posts rising to the ceiling and was draped with the same filmy net embroidered with pink rosebuds which hung at the windows. The carpet was a soft unobtrusive pink and the colour was picked up again in the deep rose-coloured satin cover that lay beneath the heavy lace bedspread.

Kate became aware that Madeau was looking at her face with an air of satisfaction but that clearly too she was expecting some comment.

'I've never seen such a lovely room, Madeau.' Although it was completely true the words were exactly those which might have been calculated to please the other woman.

'*Oui, madame.*' She walked over to the window and tweaked one of the folds of the curtain which had been displeasing her. 'And it has only just been completed. Monsieur Charles must have known,' she turned to smile admiringly at Kate, 'he must have known, although he told me nothing. Allowing me to believe . . .' She did not finish the sentence but went over to throw open a door which Kate had not noticed previously as it was painted the same soft rose colour as the walls of the room. 'And here, *madame*, is your bathroom.'

Kate smiled her pleasure as she looked round at the shining white bath, at the gold taps and at the rose-strewn white tiles. 'You know, Madeau, Monsieur Charles told me that he had some mod cons in the pigeon house and . . .'

'*Pardon, madame?*' Clearly Madeau had not understood, but before there was a chance to explain they heard the sound of Charles coming into the bedroom and moved through to join him.

'It's a beautiful room, Charles.' For once Kate kept nothing back as she stood watching him place the cases on the bench at the foot of her bed. 'Quite perfect.'

'I'm glad.' His reply was laconic, but she sensed that he too was pleased with her enthusiasm.

Madeau, her head to one side, looked at them knowingly. '*Pardon, madame*, perhaps you would like some tea.'

'That would be lovely, Madeau. I haven't had tea since I . . .' Her voice trailed away as she remembered the day of her arrival at the château.

'Then I shall go and make some. It will be ready in about fifteen minutes . . .'

'Oh, Madeau . . .' Charles interrupted her with some instructions in French which Kate who was only half listening understood to be something to do with the evening meal. She heard him talking about the Auberge and assumed that they would be going out to eat.

But Madeau would have none of that, and the last words spoken as she went out the door were final indeed. '*A deux, monsieur. Ce soir vous diniez à deux. Ici. Chez vous.*'

There was silence for a moment as the door closed firmly but quietly behind her. Then Charles walked over to the window and pulled aside the curtain. 'Have you seen the view from here?'

'No. I did hear you call it the garden room. I didn't see any garden.'

'No.' His voice was suddenly distant, unemotional. 'It lies at the side of the house.'

With a reluctance she could scarcely understand Kate walked over to stand beside him. 'Yes, it is beautiful.' She looked down on the wistaria rioting over the pergola, at the pelargoniums spilling pink and white from the huge stone urns, but she scarcely saw them, so conscious was she of the figure standing so near. And his scrutiny of her profile was beginning to bring the colour selfconsciously into her cheeks again. Desperately she searched for something to divert attention from herself and leaning forward into the window embrasure she found it.

'Oh, you have a swimming pool!' She had not meant the relief she felt to show so clearly in her manner.

'Yes.' His reply was dry and she felt a qualm when he moved away from her towards the door, but she refused to turn and look at him. 'I shall wait for you in the hall so that I can show you the rest of the house.'

'Oh yes, thank you.' Unwillingly she swung round to where he stood with his hand on the heavy brass knob of the door. 'I'll be down in a few minutes. I'll just tidy my hair.' Charles nodded briefly and the door closed soundlessly behind him.

Kate stared at the door wishing she could think of some logical explanation of the effect this man had on her. Even with the distance of the room between them she could sense some power urging her towards him, some influence that made her afraid to trust her own reactions. It couldn't simply be sex. In the frankly randy world of advertising she had always been able to handle that and had never found herself in an even vaguely threatening situation. But now, she was by no means sure of Charles Savoney-Morlet and even less so of herself. Last night she had made up her mind to do something about it, and now was the very moment when she ought to begin.

It was barely five minutes later when she found her way along the corridor and down the stair into the hall. Charles rose from a chair in a shadowy corner and threw down the letters he had been reading. For a moment Kate was afraid that he would make some comment on her altered appearance, but after a swift, not very encouraging glance at her hair which she had slicked down with oil and tied back in a rubber band he said nothing but simply led her to a door and stood back so that she could precede him.

Surprisingly the sitting-room had been done out in a completely modern style, but one that was so understated it fitted in with the rest of the house. The room was enormous and had been divided into two parts, one part of it clearly used as a work place, with a desk and some of the impedimenta of the photographer's trade about it.

But it was the other end of the room that attracted Kate's attention first, where the huge arched window filled the entire wall and which gave light not only to the sitting-room but to a second room suspended above the first and extending several yards into the centre. A flight of steps led up to a gallery with an elaborately carved balustrade leading along to this hanging room.

Kate turned round, amazed by such unusual and daring architecture, and then with a tiny shake of her head she smiled at Charles, who was watching her reactions closely.

'It's . . . quite fantastic!'

'Is that good? Or bad?' It was difficult to tell whether her reaction had pleased him.

'It's good—of course you must know that. I can't think how it all came about.'

'Well, this was a high barn when first I came. You can imagine it, can't you?' She nodded following the sweeping movements of his hand as he illustrated. 'It was full of straw when I came in and there was just an earth floor.' He tapped the golden wood with one polished brown shoe. 'And up there was a platform with some kind of ancient lifting gear on it. There was a tiny shuttered opening there and underneath there were large doors for carts to come in. When I was supervising the first alterations,' he grinned in sudden amusement as he pointed to the upper storey, 'I put a bed up there. It was then that I decided I would make that my bedroom.'

'Up there?'

'Yes, come up and see.' Without waiting to see if she were willing he walked towards the stairs and Kate despite her reluctance felt she could scarcely refuse. 'I could never bear to leave this view.' He stood at the window looking out and after a moment's hesitation she followed him, understanding instantly what he meant. Here they seemed to tower above the ground with the swimming pool a patch of blue far below, the river dizzily distant. But now in the late afternoon, with the rich summer light casting a shimmer over everything, the long slow descent to the valley with all the variety of greens and golds was sheer enchantment. Kate held her breath for a long moment before releasing it on a sigh of satisfaction.

'That I can understand.' She spoke softly, causing him to turn round swiftly towards her. 'And,' she refused to meet his gaze but turned to walk into the middle of the room, 'I like your bedroom, even though it's a bit unconventional. Don't you find it just a bit draughty in winter?'

'Not at all.' To prove his point Charles strolled over to the window and pressed a button causing the heavy tweed curtains which hung from floor to ceiling at each side of the window to come swishing smoothly across shutting out the light. Then another switch caused shutters to close over the balcony so that in an instant they were enclosed in the monastic simplicity of his bedroom.

There was a feverish expression on Kate's face as she glanced from him to the narrow bed, neat and trim with its tailored brown cover, to the row of wooden doors behind which his clothes were presumably hidden, although one opened a mere fraction to show the tiled floor and brown curtain of a shower room.

'So you see it is very . . . private, Kate. Up here you can feel quite cut away from the world.' The slanted eyes were watching her very closely. 'Don't you agree . . . *chérie*?'

'Yes.' She tried to make her voice sound brisk and sure, but with that disturbing scrutiny, found it difficult. 'Yes, I'm sure it must be.' Desperately she wrenched her gaze from his and found relief in some pencil sketches hanging on the wall close to where she knew the stairs were. 'These are effective.' Both of them were portraits of a woman—the same woman; in one her hair was loose and blowing across her face and she was smiling, and in the other it was swept into a sort of coronet. There was the impression of fairness and the eyes had a lightness that seemed to rob the face of character. In one corner Kate saw the initials C.S.C. 'A friend of yours?' She asked the question casually over her shoulder.

'Yes.' His reply was so short that she turned round to look enquiringly into his face, surprising an expression of dark brooding intensity. Then as a welcome release from the awkwardness of the moment they heard the sound of a bell ringing down below, and when Charles pressed the button the shutters slipped quickly back into their concealed alcove.

'Tea, *madame*!' Madeau called quietly, almost apologetically, and watched smiling as Kate, her cheeks burning, went quickly along the gallery and down the stairs to the sitting room.

The tray had been placed on the glass-topped coffee table and when she had assured herself that they had everything necessary Madeau closed the door and left them. Kate sat in one of the huge soft leather settees and began to busy herself with the tea things, wishing that her hands didn't shake so much when she was performing such an everyday task.

'I'm sorry,' she smiled tentatively in Charles' direction, 'I ought to know, but I don't—do you take sugar and cream?'

'No reason why you should know.' Although his tone was bland his eyes surveyed her with positive dislike. 'As you say, yesterday we hadn't even met. Just a dash of cream, no sugar.'

Kate lowered her head, refusing to allow him to guess how his manner had hurt her, and if she were honest with herself she found it hard to understand. Surely this was what she was planning, to ensure a state of antipathy between them. Till Antoine came for her.

Without speaking she held out the plate of sandwiches to him, relieved when he took several and put them on his plate, for she had just realised how hungry she felt. But when he shook his head and refused a piece of the delicious-looking gâteau Madeau had produced she decided she ought to argue with him.

'You must,' masterfully she slid the cake on to his plate and handed him a silver fork, 'or Madeau will be very disappointed.'

'Will she?' Obligingly Charles took the fork and broke off a piece of the cake. 'I doubt it. Madeau knows my tastes well enough and doesn't expect me to eat many sweet things. But if you insist then I'll try to finish it.' He pushed his cup across the table. 'And if I could have another cup of tea to help it down . . .' He waited while she filled his cup, studying her closely through narrowed eyes. 'I'm glad to see you like food, Kate, if you're to be married to a Frenchman. And you don't seem to have any of these slimming fads that so many women have.'

'Someone told me,' Kate licked the last piece of cream from her spoon, 'that it was time I lost some weight.'

'Oh?'

'Yes.' Slightly annoyed by his lack of comment, she found herself stammering. 'It was . . . someone at work.'

'You've no need. To slim, I mean.'

'Oh!' The colour flooded into her cheeks as she realised that she had been waiting for a compliment, expecting it even. That much must have been obvious to him. And he had, albeit minimally, paid it.

With a bang Kate replaced her plate on the tray beside her cup and saucer and got to her feet. She wandered about the room, looking at the pictures on the walls, mostly modern, vibrant with colour and giving an impression of light. They were framed in heavy brass which suited their uncompromising impressionism.

All the time she was conscious of Charles's eyes following her, making her feel awkward, a stranger, an interloper. Her eyes lighted on a group of photographs arranged in a block on one wall of the studio end of the room.

'May I?' She gestured towards them.

'Of course.' He shrugged, then rose to his feet, going over to press a switch so that the walls were flooded with soft light.

Kate walked over, her eyes narrowing in surprise as she saw some studies of a famous New York model.

'It's Auriol Hayden, isn't it?' Then when there was no reply she turned round to look at him. 'Isn't it?' she demanded.

'Yes.'

'Gosh!' Hastily she scrutinised the rest of the photographs, noticing the quality of the camera work, the softness of the outlines, the way the light caught the downy hair of the girl's face before her eyes went to the signature black and bold in one corner. 'Charles Saint Cyr.' She spoke the name with wonder and admiration. 'For heaven's sake, they're by Charles Saint Cyr! Did you know?' She flashed an excited glance in the direction of the silent man who stood dark and shadowy behind her.

He didn't reply, but she searched the rows of photographs, uttering little cries of admiration. 'Isn't she gorgeous? And isn't he the most marvellous . . .' She stopped when she caught sight of another photograph, one on its own and unframed, tucked into the dark frame of one of the more important pictures.

It took her a moment to recognise the man in the photograph. He was sitting back in his chair and laughing. And the girl who was leaning forward over their restaurant table, touching his cheek with her long tinted fingers, was the most famous model in the United

States. But there was no doubt about it, and the realisation brought a cold trickle to her spine. Slowly she turned round to face him.

'You should have told me.' Her voice was flat, dispirited.

'Told you what, *chérie*?'

'Oh, nothing at all.' Now she wanted to lash him with her sarcasm. 'Telling me that you took photographs. Why didn't you tell me that you were Charles Saint Cyr? Did you think that I might pester you for a job?'

It took him a long time to answer and while she waited Kate trembled with the emotion that seemed to stretch tautly between them.

'No, that idea was one that hadn't occurred to me. I simply thought that perhaps it would be best to get to know each other slowly. For instance, there are things that you haven't told me. Such as why you did such a mad thing as come to a country where you understand little of the language to marry a man you don't know. And why you don't even have the sense to bring a friend with you. Does your family care so little for you that none of this matters?'

'How dare you speak to me like that!' The violet eyes blazed with sudden fury, fanned by the realisation that no one could dispute the sense that lay behind his questions. 'How dare you, when you,' she repeated the accusation on a rising note, '*you* have taken part in a deception that must even in this country be beyond the law! What would your position be, Monsieur Saint Cyr or Savoney-Morlet—it's hard to know who you really are—if I went to the police and told them all about the farce yesterday? You *and* your aunt would, I suspect, find yourselves in jail!'

'But you've no intention of going to the police, have you, Kate?' He had taken a step towards her and stood looking down, eyes narrowed menacingly. Then a hand snaked out, catching her, not very gently, by the wrist and pulling her against him. 'If you had, then you had lots of opportunity today when we stopped in Lioran to buy the things for lunch. You passed a policeman, and don't tell me you didn't notice him, because I saw you smile at each other.'

Kate coloured indignantly. 'Of course I didn't! At least, when he nodded . . .'

'Of course,' he jeered. 'You had to respond, but still it would make any complaints to the police difficult to support when you came running back so eagerly to the car. It would seem strange in view of the complaint you would be making.'

'Let go of my arm!' The words were hissed between clenched teeth. 'You're hurting!'

Suddenly, although his cruel grip on her wrist was released, she found herself clasped to him in a more tender, infinitely more agreeable embrace, his hands sliding round her waist, then over her hips, moulding her pliant body irresistibly against his. Startled blue eyes looked up, bewildered, into the now blatantly mocking dark ones.

'Don't worry, Kate, there's nothing personal in the least about this. It's just that I hear Madeau coming and . . .' But he said no more, for just then his mouth, undeniable, searching, took possession of hers, expertly parting her lips with his own, sending the flames licking through her veins with unquenchable power.

But just as she allowed herself to be carried along in the spell of bewildering delight, as she felt the tumult of passion begin to overwhelm her senses as well as her body, it was snatched away from her and Charles was holding her at arm's length, physically and mentally.

'*Pardon, madame*—Monsieur Charles.' With a smile that showed no embarrassment, only understanding, Madeau hurried out of the room carrying the tea tray and the door closed again behind her.

Kate found the passion of a second before supplanted by an overwhelming contempt for herself and for Charles, but for the moment she was too shaken to express her feelings. Instead she leaned against the desk, oblivious of the rapid rise and fall of her bosom, conscious only of the anguish that racked her body. If she had been less involved with her own feelings she might have seen that his face was pale and disturbed beneath the suntan. Furiously she felt the prick of tears behind her eyes and knew that if she did not escape she was in danger of allowing him to see her feelings. Hurriedly she thrust herself away from the desk and rushed towards the door.

'Damn you!' She paused with her hand on the knob. 'Damn you!' The sob rose in her throat and she was unable to control it.

It was only when she reached the sanctuary of her bedroom that she was able to regain control of her own emotions to begin to think clearly. Charles Saint Cyr. She should have known, of course. That was why from the first she had seen something vaguely familiar in their features. First Antoine, and now Charles. She had seen his photograph often enough in fashion magazines in the past.

Charles Saint Cyr—a name that was mentioned in the same breath as Bailey and Snowdon. Internationally famous for fashion, society portraits, seen constantly in the company of beautiful women. So what was she doing here with him? Distractedly she put her clenched fist to her mouth, pressing her teeth down on her fingers in the hope that the pain would blot out his image from her mind.

But it didn't. Her mind was filled with tortured imaginings about him and Auriol Hayden, and Kate could scarcely avoid the implication that what she was feeling was nothing other than jealousy. It was all too ridiculous, of course. But dangerous. She had seen that look in his eyes, and she knew the response of her own emotions. The sooner she did something about both, the better it would be . . .

CHAPTER FIVE

It was difficult always to be wholly satisfied with life. If that was true in the most ordinary circumstances how much more obvious it was in her present position. Kate reflected on the perversity of human nature as she got up from bed and went to the bathroom for her shower.

Who would have thought a few days ago when she embarked on her programme of discouraging Charles that she would have been disappointed by the ease with which she had succeeded? For after that first day, when for Madeau's benefit he had kissed her, he had treated her with absolute, uninvolved correctness.

She sighed as she stepped out of the stream of warm water and reached for a towel. A kiss—it sounded so simple, such an everyday occurrence, and yet it had shaken the very basis of her beliefs, her understanding of the male–female relationship. It had all been easy before, to fall in love, to marry and to live happily ever after. There should be none of this tearing, utterly exhausting emotion. And there should be no need for a girl idyllically in love with one man, with Antoine, to be so conscious of another.

Kate stood in front of the mirror and sprayed her hair with sun-filter oil, then brushing it fiercely into the least attractive style she could manage she secured it with an elastic band, adding a few kirbigrips above her ears to contain the few wisps which had an annoying inclination to escape and to curl.

Dressed in her pants and bra, she walked over to the cupboards which now were fairly well filled with all the lovely clothes she had bought for her honeymoon. She sighed as she surveyed the colourful array of cotton and silk dresses. It seemed such a pity when the sun had been shining so gloriously since she had come, but . . . Resolutely she thrust her indecision from her and reached for the navy jeans and the mud-coloured blouse which she had bought in an underlit boutique in Chelsea.

There, Kate, she told herself when she was ready, that should subdue any interest Charles might have in your beautiful body. Then with a wry little smile she reminded herself that Charles had shown few signs of wanting to ravish her. Even that first night, when Madeau had prepared a delicious dinner to celebrate, he had shown no sign of having noticed his wife's passionate attachment to jeans and a blouse.

That faint raising of the eyebrows when he saw her come downstairs might have been imagination, not the fact that he disapproved of her slicked-down hair or her casual dress. He certainly didn't subscribe to her dressing-down ethic, for he was quite devastating in dark slacks and a plum-coloured velvet jacket with a snowy shirt front. But Kate suspected that Madeau was more disappointed in the lack of dress sense shown by the new Madame Savoney-Morlet than was Charles himself.

Only yesterday when she had come in to tidy up the already immaculate bedroom, she had lingered by the open door of the wardrobe, her fingers touching the hem of a flame-coloured cotton admiringly.

'You like trousers, *madame*?'

'Yes.' There was a hint of defiance in Kate's manner as she answered. 'I find them much more practical.'

'Ah, practical. *Oui*.' Madeau shrugged and closed the door. '*Mais pas jolis*.'

Kate didn't answer, uncertain whether Madeau's comment referred to the trousers or to herself. Further pangs of regret struck her as she faced her own reflection, then she turned away and ran downstairs to the dining room before she could be tempted to change her mind.

Charles was as always sitting at the small table by the window, but obligingly, as if she were a stranger, he got up and pulled out a chair for her. Somehow the formality irritated Kate more than usual, but she tried to hide her impatience.

'You really ought not to do that, Charles.' She glanced across at him before reaching for the tall coffee pot on the small hot stand, trying to ignore the tremor of excitement that each sight of him seemed to bring.

'Do what?' he asked coldly, picking up the newspaper he had discarded when she came into the room, although she suspected he understood exactly what she meant.

'You shouldn't get up each time I come into the room. Especially when I know you've been reading.'

'Thank you.' He picked up the paper again and turned his attention to it again. 'I'll remember.'

Kate glared at the printed pages which he raised like a barricade between them, then concentrated on peeling one of the peaches from the basket in the centre of the table. She was about to spread a roll with butter and refill her cup when there was a rustling from the seat opposite and Charles tossed the paper down on to the floor.

'More coffee?' She raised an eyebrow and held out her hand.

'*Oui. Merci.*' He handed his cup over, then as he thoughtfully stirred it he spoke again. 'I've been thinking, Kate, that really you ought to do something about learning the language. It's no good putting it off just because I and Madeau are able to speak English. It will help you to hold your own with my aunt if you have some command of French, and besides, Antoine will expect . . .'

'I'm glad you spoke of Antoine . . .' Her voice shook slightly and she replaced her cup in her saucer with care. 'I want to know just where he is, what is he doing . . .' her voice rose, showing her agitation, '. . . and why hasn't he been in contact with me?'

Charles's lips tightened. 'These are questions I cannot answer, Kate. I rang his office yesterday and . . .'

'You rang? Then why didn't you tell me? It seems I'm the last person to be told! If Antoine is in Hamburg he could at least . . .'

'Hamburg? Why should you think he's in Hamburg?' The thin dark eyebrows frowned over the watchful eyes.

'Because he told me so. When he rang me in London, the day before I left, he said he had been delayed in Hamburg and that he would be home late on the night before our wedding.' Appealingly Kate looked at the stern-faced man sitting opposite, longing for him to confirm what she had regarded as the truth.

'Antoine is not in Hamburg.' Abruptly he got up and

left the table, standing in the open french window so that his back was all that she could see. 'As far as I know he has not been there recently.'

'Then if he's not in Hamburg, where is he?'

'As far as I know, Kate,' his voice was as impassive as the back of his head, 'Antoine is in Australia.'

'Australia . . .?' The word was a mere whisper. 'But . . .'

'Listen, Kate.' Suddenly Charles swung round, sat down where he had been before and reached across the table to clasp her hands. 'Antoine has gone there to study the wine-making areas in the Barossa valley. His mother has some plans for investing money there and that's her reason for sending him. It's supposed to be for three months, but . . .'

'Three months!' Kate pulled one of her hands from his and covered her face. 'How can I bear it? Three months!'

'Don't despair, *chérie*.' When at last he spoke there was a bleakness about his voice that made her raise her eyes to search his face but it was as uninformative as ever, until a faint smile touched the corner of his mouth. 'His plan was for him to come home in the interval, and when I say home I mean France, not the château, that he would take you off my hands,' his smile widened to show that he was teasing, 'and that you would walk hand in hand into the sunset.'

'And does he imagine,' passionately she threw the question at him, 'that what has happened won't have altered anything? That I'll still feel the same? That I'll be able to trust him?'

'Yes, I think he imagines just that. He told me that nothing could alter the way you felt for each other. And think, Kate—what he is proposing to do for you is something quite special. He is preparing to defy his mother, to trick her, so that he can marry you.'

'But he shouldn't have had to,' Kate answered rather sadly. 'He should just have told her that he was going to be married, not tangle us all up in this web.'

'But I've told you, Kate, Antoine is a gentle person, too willing to think of other people's points of view. Too anxious to save people worry and anxiety . . .'

'All except me!' Her interruption was sharp.

'No. Truly he was desperately worried about you. And you mustn't blame him for not being more force-ful with his mother. After all, you thought there was something romantic about being secretive, about marrying without your mother's knowledge. Some of the fault is yours.'

'I shouldn't have told you that.' Almost as soon as she had reached her own room the first night she regretted the confidences she had poured into his listening ear, all a result of that glass of cognac he had insisted she drink with her coffee. 'And you shouldn't be reminding me of it now.'

'No. Of course you're right, Kate.' He grinned at her with no sign of regret and got up, releasing her hand from his warm comforting clasp. 'But now,' he glanced at the slim gold watch on his wrist, 'there are one or two things I must do in town. Would you like to come with me, or can you fill in an hour or two on your own?'

'I shall be all right,' she answered quickly, for she knew exactly what she meant to do the first time she had the house and garden to herself. 'I can write some letters. But,' she hesitated uncertain whether she was ready for any further revelations, 'you said you rang

Antoine's office . . .'

'*Oui*. And the reason why I said nothing is that I could find out no details of his whereabouts. He told me he'd leave details of his hotel and a number where he could be found, but according to his secretary, who incidentally is another of Madame's protégées, he is travelling around and she has no firm address. That might be true or it might not. But anyway, when he has some plans he knows this number well enough and there will be no problem. Forgive me if I rush now, *chérie*. I have an appointment with my solicitor and must go.'

Briefly he brushed his mouth against her cheek, but it was so fleeting that Kate knew it was merely a duty, that he had been unaware of the sudden flare of emotion that any contact between them was sure to arouse. And a moment later she was staring out into the courtyard, seeing the long sleek car being reversed out of the garage, then accelerating away from the house, under the arch and disappearing. Kate rushed to the sitting-room just in time to catch a glimpse of the roof of the car as it raced downhill.

Then, feeling curiously lighthearted, she ran upstairs, tore off all her clothes and quickly shampooed her hair under the shower. How pleasant it was to feel it shiny and clean again, to get rid of the unpleasant sticky texture caused by the suntan oil. When she went to the shops she must buy some other oil that would be more suitable for her disguise.

Meantime, she struggled into one of the new bathing suits she had bought for the intended honeymoon in Greece, gave herself an approving little smile in the mirror and went downstairs.

'Madeau,' she poked her head into the kitchen first. 'I'll do my room later, I want to do some sunbathing before the sun gets too hot. Then I'll have a quick swim before Monsieur Charles comes back.'

'*Oui, madame.*' Madeau turned round from the sink where she was washing some vegetables, then looked again, her eyes widening in surprise and pleasure. '*Oh, madame, si jolie!*'

'I'm glad you like it, Madeau. I'm quite pleased with it myself.'

'*Mais oui.* You look so . . . different, *madame.*'

Kate blushed, knowing just how much of a transformation this was from her usual appearance in drab jeans and blouses, and she was well aware how this clinging material emphasised the natural contours of her figure, showing the smallness of her waist and the satisfactory curves. Besides, it was a very pretty style with its black and white checkerboard design and the single strap coming up from the inverted vee under her chin.

'But I am glad, *madame,*' Madeau was looking at her rather anxiously in a way that Kate knew had little to do with her swimsuit, 'to be talking to you.'

'Yes, Madeau?' Curiously Kate looked at the woman, noticing the faint colour in her cheeks and the way her fingers played with the corner of her white apron. She had a sudden urgent fear that Madeau might be thinking of giving notice, that she no longer wanted to go on working for Charles now that he had a wife to disrupt the smooth household arrangements. 'Yes, Madeau?' she prompted again.

'I am hoping that you will speak with Monsieur Charles, tell him . . .'

Kate's heart sank farther.

'. . . You see, *madame*, we have been here so long and now . . . Now, *madame*, that I find myself *enceinte* . . .'

'You find yourself what?' Kate was bewildered.

'I am to have a baby, *madame*,' Madeau blushed. 'So unexpected. After so many childless years we had ceased to hope and . . .'

'But that's wonderful news, Madeau!' Kate smiled in relief as much as in pleasure. 'I'm sure Georges must be delighted. And you, of course.'

'*Naturellement, madame*.' A tiny frown on her face betrayed some continuing anxiety. 'But we are also concerned that Monsieur Charles will no longer want us here. It may be inconvenient with a child and . . .'

'Oh no, I'm sure you're wrong, Madeau. I can't imagine Charles . . .' Kate paused, suddenly aware that she might be taking too much on herself.

But Madeau noticed none of her hesitation, her expression showing a relief that explained the extent of her previous anxiety. 'Oh, *madame*, I told Georges it would be so. I said now that Monsieur Charles has Madame he can do with a little less of my time. You like the work, *madame*, already I can see that, the way you keep your room and help round the house. So will you explain to Monsieur Charles for me?'

'Of course I will, Madeau.' As Kate pulled the sunglasses down from the top of her head and went out to lie on a seat by the side of the pool there was a thoughtful expression on her face.

But the beauty, the sheer perfection of the day was enough to dispel any anxiety she felt about Charles's reception of the news. Soon the worries, her own even more than those concerned with Madeau, began to float away as the sun's kiss began to ease the pain that had reached into her very bones. She stirred once, reaching up a languorous hand to adjust the position of the sun umbrella so that her face and shoulders were partly shaded and again to slide back the lounger and find a more comfortable position for her head on the pillow. Just for the moment such perfect comfort was all she asked of life.

Kate had no idea how long she slept or what it was that woke her. It might have been the enticing clink of ice against glass, possibly the shadow, soundless though it was, passing between her reclining body and the life-giving sun. Whatever it was her eyes shot open suddenly, her heart palpitated as she gazed up at the tall dark shape.

'Sorry, *chérie*,' as she watched him, Charles pulled at the tie round the neck of his cream silk shirt and began to undo the buttons, 'I moved the shade in case the sun should be too much for you. I didn't mean to disturb you. You looked so . . . *tranquille* lying there.'

Finding the combination of his intense gaze and the exposure of tanned skin too disturbing to conceal, Kate swung her legs on to the ground, reaching at once for the sunglasses she had thrown on to the table before lying down.

'No, I had no intention of sleeping.' She stood up, taller than usual in her cork-soled sandals with the thong ties round her ankles. 'I thought you would be away for hours.' There was a note of accusation in her voice which might have been the reason for the wry smile that twisted his lips.

'I think we may have had the same idea, Kate. I found the prospect of a swim in the pool very appealing. Not,' he pulled his shirt free from his slacks as he spoke but never took his mocking eyes from her face, 'not that I imagined I would be lucky enough to have the company of my beautiful wife. Sit down, Kate.' He nodded towards the seat she had just vacated. 'I persuaded Madeau to make us a jug of fresh orange juice. Let me pour a glass for you.'

'No, really, I've been out too long already.' She wondered if he heard the note of panic in her voice. 'I promised I would help inside. Besides . . .' she touched the skin of her shoulders gently, '. . . I don't want to get too much sun at once or I might begin to peel.'

'Mmm.' He followed the direction of her fingers, then put out his hand to touch her, slowly tracing the line of the deeply cut armholes. 'I don't think there's any danger.' He spoke so impassively that she could only conclude that he had felt nothing of the tingling excited throb his touch had brought to her. 'Sit down, Kate,' he said again, and now her knees felt so weak that she had little choice but to subside into her chair.

'Drink this.' The glass he handed to her was cool, the shiver of ice inviting, and she was grateful for the thirst-quenching sharpness of the fruit. Charles pulled a chair close to hers, so that they were sitting almost touching, facing each other. Kate tried to think of something noncommittal to say.

'You finished your business?'

'Yes, I got through it much quicker than I thought I would. And as I said, I couldn't get back to you fast enough, Kate.' His eyes travelled in a leisurely, appreciative way over her lightly clad figure. 'I must say I much prefer this outfit to the one you usually wear. And your hair.' He looked at the silky golden-brown cloud that touched her shoulders.

Kate ignored his comments, although it was impossible for her to control the colour that stained her cheeks, a phenomenon which he noticed with a sardonic smile. A rapid change of subject was in order, so she said the first thing she could think of. 'Did Madeau say anything to you?'

'Madeau?' He shook his head. 'What about?'

Kate fixed her eyes on his face, wishing she could exclude from her vision that dark smooth chest with the spray of dark hair, wishing it didn't force itself into her consciousness with such blatant sexuality. 'She didn't say anything about the baby?'

'The baby?' His eyes came together in a sudden angry frown and his feet which he had casually stretched out on to a cane stool hit the ground in an expression of his barely controlled fury.

'Baby!' He snapped the word at her, at the same time sweeping her figure with a penetrating glance. 'For God's sake, why didn't you tell me?'

'Tell you?' The colour drained from her cheeks, leaving her white and shaken. There was no doubt in her mind that he had totally misunderstood, and she felt indignation and a quite unreasonable hurt although she tried to answer calmly. 'Why on earth should I tell you that Madeau is pregnant?'

'Madeau?' For a moment he stared at her before visibly relaxing and then grinning with a relief that he didn't trouble to hide. 'Oh, for a moment I thought ...'

'I'm perfectly well aware of the way your mind works.' Carefully Kate replaced her empty glass on the table, at the same time swinging her legs to the ground and standing. 'But now I'm going inside to write those letters and . . .'

'No, Kate—wait!' Charles had got to his feet with one easy move, reaching out a hand to clasp her wrist. There was a lazy smile at his lips, the dark eyes glinted mischievously as they tried to penetrate the smoked glass hiding her eyes. 'You gave me a shock. I jumped to the wrong conclusion, that's all.'

'You would,' she said with a coldness that belied the torment his touch brought. 'Anyway, Madeau is concerned about the situation. She seems to think you'll give them notice now that she's having a baby, and . . .'

'I don't believe Madeau said any such thing.' He seemed amused rather than annoyed at her implication of his intolerance. 'And if it will soften that disapproving expression, be assured that I'm delighted about Madeau and Georges. And their baby.'

'You didn't seem to be delighted when first I mentioned it.'

'Ah, but then, Kate, I thought that you . . .'

'I know what you thought . . .' Her words had a hint of wildness about them. 'But why should you care? If it had been my baby why should it have mattered to you?'

'That I don't know, Kate.' There was a stillness about him, a watchfulness about his dark face as he answered. 'I only know it would have mattered to me— a great deal.' He ignored her hasty, weak attempt to wrest her wrist from his strong grasp, diverting her attention by putting up a hand to take the sunglasses from her eyes. 'You know, Kate,' his tone was reflective as if his interest were professional rather than personal, 'you should never hide those eyes behind smoked glass. It's a pity to deprive the rest of us of the pleasure.'

Kate's swift attempt to snatch at the glasses was

thwarted as he laughingly held them at arm's length. 'Please,' she asked in a tone of thinly veiled anger, 'would you give them back to me?'

'Why, Kate?' Now he was jeering. 'So you can hide behind them again? What are you afraid of? Why do you wear the ugliest clothes you can find and pull back your hair so that you look like some old washerwoman?'

'How dare you!' she gasped, jerked out of her cool control by his unflattering comparison.

'Why, Kate?' His voice softened, bringing the treacherous sliding weakness she feared so much. 'When you can look as you did lying asleep on that chair? So beautiful, my Kate, that a man could lose himself in you.' As he spoke he reached up his hand, touching her hair, trickling his fingers down over her shoulder, holding her chin firmly so that there was no escape from his searching eyes. 'Why, Kate?' he asked softly.

Unable to wrench her gaze from his, Kate tried to collect her thoughts, made an effort to resist the longing to relax against that broad chest, to spread her fingers over the warm skin and then at last to raise her mouth to his. 'Why?' she echoed woodenly, trying to ignore the tumult of desire that was threatening to absorb and control her entire body. 'Because,' she closed her eyes, determined to exclude his disturbing masculinity at least from her vision, 'because I thought it would have been clear enough—I think of it as a penance.'

'A penance?' It was obvious that she had caught him on the raw, and that fact gave her strength enough to open her eyes.

'Yes, a penance. Which I will give up only when I see Antoine again.'

'I see.' As he spoke the words reflectively, apparently debating whether or not her answer was a credible one, his hand dropped from her chin and he released her arm. And strangely Kate, who an instant before had been so anxious to escape, lost all inclination to do so. 'I see,' Charles repeated. 'But you must be careful, Kate. For should you overdo it, you might find that if Antoine comes back unexpectedly he won't recognise you as the beautiful girl he fell in love with in London.'

'I don't think there's any danger.'

'Of course there isn't.' He smiled at her again, then reached out for her glasses which he had dropped on to the table and perched them on her nose. 'But now I think I'll join you in a swim.' He bent to pick up his shirt from the chair. 'You'll wait till I change?'

'All right.' Kate had had no intention of being so amenable, but even when Charles turned towards the house she couldn't quite make up her mind to run upstairs and shut herself in her bedroom. Besides, she made the excuse, knowing that she was being dishonest with herself, the water, dazzling blue and limpidly inviting, would have the same effect as a cold shower.

Charles was as powerful a swimmer as she would have imagined for a man with his physique, but as it was the one sport at which she excelled Kate felt no diffidence about her own performance. She knew that he had to slacken his pace to suit hers as they stroked up and down the length of the pool, but when he began to toss about the large ball which had been lying on the surface, she relaxed, forgot about her tensions as she stroked with her powerful overarm crawl in pursuit of it.

'You're quite a girl,' he grinned at her as, insisting that she was exhausted, she climbed the short flight of steps at the corner of the pool.

'Yes?' The implied compliment pleased her, and she smiled, breathlessly pushing back from her face the strands of sodden hair.

'Yes.' The slash of white in his dark face disappeared slowly, his hand came out linking round her neck, pulling her irresistibly against him. 'Kate.' His voice was incredibly low and deep, his eyes dark and sensuous.

She quivered slightly, unable to move away from him yet wholly aware of the danger implicit in their closeness. A hand moved to her waist, sliding down to where the plunging back of her suit ended. It was strange to shiver when this burning fevered excitement possessed her. With a fluttering little sigh she allowed herself to be pulled against him, felt the pressure of his limbs against hers, at last able to spread her fingers over the cool dampness of his skin.

'Kate.' Softly spoken, half groan, half triumphant declaration, her name seemed to linger on his lips. 'Kate, *chérie*.'

His hands tightened about her, their bodies longed to merge, and their lips. The dark-fringed lids dropped over the violet eyes, yet she saw his mouth moving towards hers, the teeth gleamed as his mouth parted to enclose hers.

And then there was the sound of heels tapping sharply on the tiled paving at the side of the house. They heard Madeau speak, followed by another, a lighter, more brittle female voice. Brutally, painfully, Kate found herself thrust away, heard a muttered imprecation from Charles before he turned in a sudden dive to resurface at the furthest corner of the pool. Kate stood, feeling the blood drain from her heart. It was as if the world had been unexpectedly offered to her on a plate. And as suddenly snatched away.

CHAPTER SIX

BLINDLY Kate reached for the rope handle at the side of the steps and with its support was able to drag herself out of the water to stand, feeling faintly sick, on the side of the pool. At the far end she could see Madeau lean over the water to say something to Charles. Madeau had a slightly worried expression on her face, but Charles was looking beyond her to a figure standing by the table. Kate watched him smile, then with a single lithe move heave himself from the pool and walk casually, arrogantly over to the immaculately dressed woman who leaned forward to kiss his lips.

Madeau had disappeared before Kate heard her name and came out of the trance into which she had dropped. Numbly she watched the two people walk towards her, the tall dark man dressed only in brief black swimming trunks and the woman whose blonde hair gleamed with a silvery light in the sunshine.

'Kate,' he was smiling as if the interruption of that intimate moment in the pool had meant nothing to him, 'come and meet Françoise.'

Summoning some courage which she hadn't known she possessed, twisting her lips into what might have passed for a smile, Kate stepped forward. She tried not to shudder as Charles draped an amiable arm about her shoulders, turning her to face the visitor. The woman wore fashionably huge sunglasses, but they did not quite conceal the narrowing of her eyes as she noted the gesture.

'This is Françoise,' Charles drew her closer with a possessive little gesture as he smiled down at the top of her head. 'She and her family have been my friends since I first arrived, a penniless refugee.' He looked straight—challengingly? Kate wondered—at the fair girl. 'This is Kate. She and I were married just a few days ago.'

Kate wondered if she had been the only one to hear the swiftly indrawn breath, to see how the bright red lips tightened, the lower one caught briefly, fiercely between small white teeth.

'Married?' Her tone, her laugh were masterly in their control. There was a short fraught silence. 'But how wonderfully romantic!' She spoke English well and with a charming accent which made one forget that her voice was high and rather shrill. 'Charles,' with a slender pink-tipped finger she tapped him reprovingly on the chest, 'how could you be so secretive? Why should you hide your bride away?' Her eyes travelled slowly over Kate as if she expected to find an answer to her question there. 'When your friends would be so . . . interested to see her.'

'I haven't done that.' There was the hint of relief in Charles's manner as if some interview he had been dreading was safely over. 'But as I said, Kate and I have been married less than a week.' Again he touched the top of her head with his cheek—in case, thought Kate mutinously, Françoise should not get the message. The very idea made her blush, and that too would be seen as significant.

'Well, if you'll excuse me,' she murmured as she stepped away from the protective arm, 'I think I'd better go and put on some clothes.'

'Of course,' Françoise waved an understanding hand. 'I shall keep all my questions till you come down.'

'And I'll try to persuade Françoise to stay to lunch, darling.' Kate half turned as she reached the corner, glad that the woman had her back turned so that she could safely glare at her husband.

'Lovely,' she said sweetly, but made sure that her poisonous look would leave him in no doubt as to her real feelings.

Kate shook the bottle of suntan oil viciously as she stood in front of the bathroom mirror. She couldn't explain the antipathy she had felt for their visitor. It couldn't have anything to do with the pencil drawings she had seen on Charles's bedroom wall, even though now she had met the subject. Françoise had styled her hair differently since they had been done, of course, and Kate didn't think the cap of curls suited her as well. It made her look older. And since she was at least thirty, surely that wasn't an effect she wanted.

Anyway, Kate decided with a sour little grin at her reflection as she sprinkled the oil over her still damp hair, when she sees me at lunchtime it will do wonders for her morale! She searched in her wardrobe for her oldest pair of jeans and wasn't satisfied with a blouse until she had found one that had been too dry when she had run a hasty iron over it just before leaving London.

The way Charles's eyebrows had drawn together in an angry frown as well as the curving of Françoise's mouth assured her of the wisdom of her choice. She pretended not to notice the first and responded with enthusiasm to the second as she put out a hand to take the glass which Charles held out on a tray.

'Please,' she waved her hand dramatically, ignoring the way the sherry slopped over her jeans, 'please go on talking in French.' She held up the little book she had brought downstairs with her. 'I'll try to follow the conversation. And if there's a word I can't understand then you can wait while I look it up.'

'I'm afraid, *chérie*,' Charles was a study in loving patience, 'that you're condemning us to a silent lunch. That book will be of no use to you. I think until we have some lessons arranged for you it would be best if we stuck to English. I'm sure Françoise won't mind.'

'No, but I insist.' Kate lay back on the sofa, stretching out one foot on to the cushion where the grubby sneakers she was wearing would be sure to attract attention. 'Go ahead.' And warming to the part she was taking, she took a large noisy gulp from her glass. Françoise's look of satisfied contempt was all Kate could have hoped for, but something, a tiny shiver of fear, made her refrain from checking her husband's reaction.

There was no doubt about Madeau's disappointment as she announced lunch, nor mistaking the tiny disapproving look she gave the blouse as she placed the slices of chilled melon in front of them as they sat round the large circular table in the dining room. Kate saw her smile faintly at Françoise, a smile that reminded her of a mother's unspoken plea for indulgence when her child was misbehaving. She blushed, and the other woman's self-satisfied smile did nothing to reassure.

Not that Françoise was wrong to be pleased with her own appearance. The pink linen suit that fitted her slender figure so snugly must have cost the earth. Kate, with her inside experience of the fashion trade, knew just how much some women were prepared to spend on clothes, and that first glance confirmed Françoise in the extravagantly well-heeled category. The suit, the matching cream kid handbag and sandals, everything about her, the sunglasses, the perfume, even the tiny lace handkerchief which she put to the tip of her small straight nose, all shrieked money.

It didn't make her beautiful. Without being particularly bitchy Kate could admit that. Her eyes were too light, a pale almost transparent green which might have been striking with dark hair, but with her almost white fairness they made her face seem insignificant. Although Charles seemed to disagree with her assessment. Enough to do sketches, enough to want to hang them in his bedroom. Kate looked up suddenly, realising that Françoise was expecting an answer to some question she had asked.

'I'm sorry . . .' Kate coloured and at once felt gauche. How this woman must be laughing at her! 'I'm sorry, Françoise, I didn't quite hear . . .

'I was asking . . .' Françoise darted an amused glance at her host, '. . . how you like the idea of being married to a famous photographer. Will you find the fashion world very frightening?'

'No,' Kate couldn't resist the opportunity to score a faint triumph, 'I don't think so.' She lowered her eyes demurely, seeing her fingers playing with the stem of her glass. 'I'm quite used to it.'

'Used to it?' Gaped would have been an unkind word, but it was the one Kate thought of when she saw Françoise's expression.

'Yes.' Kate flicked a glance at Charles, intrigued to see the beginning of a smile on his lips. 'I work in fashion.'

'You . . .' Françoise could not stop her eyes from wandering over what was visible of Kate's disreputable clothing. 'You're *in* fashion?' Her tone implied that there were all sorts of ways of being in fashion, but before she could ask any more Kate, suddenly the attentive hostess, leaned forward, offering the salad bowl.

'No. No, thank you.' There was a faintly bemused expression on her face when she turned to Charles. 'Well, now that the secret is out, Charles, when are you going to invite all your friends to meet your wife?' The colourless eyes slid round to look at Kate with satisfaction. 'I'm sure they'd all love to see her.'

'I've been thinking of that myself, Françoise,' Charles said smoothly with hardly a glance in his wife's direction, 'and I have decided that it isn't fair to keep her to myself any longer. Saturday night will suit us perfectly, so we hope to see you then. Isn't that so, darling?' And the look he turned on Kate was filled with challenge. And amusement.

'Of course,' Kate bared her teeth in his direction, taking advantage of Françoise's averted head, 'darling.' Her sarcastic drawl had the apparent effect of increasing his amusement and the visitor darted a suspicious, jealous glance at Kate.

'I've just had an idea.' Charles looked from one to the other of them. 'If I can persuade Françoise, that is.'

'That shouldn't be too difficult,' Kate interrupted sweetly, then in response to the sour glance the other girl gave, 'You seem so easy-going, Françoise.'

'We've been talking about French lessons for you, Kate, then perhaps Françoise would agree to take you in hand. It would also have the advantage of helping you two girls to get to know each other.'

There was a moment's stunned silence which Charles seemed unaware of. Kate felt her mind whirling round in search of a credible excuse and she was fairly certain that Françoise would be undergoing a similar experience. In the event it was the guest who first managed to find the right words.

'Oh, that would be fascinating, Charles. But unfortunately I expect to be away from home rather a lot in the next few weeks—and I expect you will be in the same situation.' She smiled insincerely across at Kate. 'How does the prospect of going to New York suit you?'

'New York?' Kate stalled for time, her eyes going to Charles in a silent appeal.

'Kate doesn't know yet about New York,' he interrupted smoothly. 'I've been keeping it as a surprise. But as you've mentioned it, Françoise,' he shrugged philsophically, 'in ten days I'm flying to the States, *chérie*, and of course you're coming with me.' He turned to explain to their guest. 'Kate's mother is based in New York and we're hoping that she'll be there when we go there. But as soon as possible we want to set off on our delayed honeymoon.' His eyes lingered lovingly on Kate's pink cheeks, but he missed the spots of high colour in the other woman's face. 'Perhaps we may go on to somewhere more glamorous when I've finished. Where would you like to go, *chérie*?' He leaned one elbow on the table supporting his chin with forefinger and thumb as he searched her face. 'Mexico, Bali?

Somewhere warm where we can laze on the beach all day and dance all . . .'

'And what about Auriol?' Françoise's interruption was smooth, her feelings only betrayed by the tightness of her lips. 'Do you expect to see her this time?'

'I think that is inevitable. And of course I'm looking forward to seeing her again. She's one of my best friends, after all.'

Soon they finished lunch and Kate stood with Charles's arm round her shoulders watching while Françoise got into the small red sports car and started the engine. 'I shall see you on Saturday, then.' She adjusted the black and pink silk square about her head, waved a casual arm and shot through the archway, out of the courtyard.

At once and without further speaking Kate removed herself from her husband's encircling arm, reaching the stairs before his voice speaking her name firmly made her pause, one raised foot on the first step, her hand on the polished banister.

'Yes?' Facing him defiantly over her shoulder, she was conscious of the sorry contrast they made, he dressed in lightweight beige slacks and a black open-necked shirt, casual but immaculate, and she . . . Well, she didn't want to think how she looked. But it appeared that she wasn't to be allowed to forget it.

'I am asking you not to wear any of those disgusting clothes again. They . . .'

'You're what?' Amused incredulity was the only defence she could think of, and it had the secondary benefit of smothering her feelings of guilt. As she advanced up the stairs she gave a dismissive condescending little laugh, pleased when she saw Charles's features immediately darken.

'Kate.' He stepped forward, putting his hand over hers as it lay on the rail. 'If you want me to express myself more firmly then I'm forbidding you to wear them.'

'Don't,' she snapped at him between her teeth, 'don't forbid me to do anything! You have no right. And besides, I don't like it.'

'Be damned to what you like!' He removed his touch from hers, stood back with his hands low on his hips, looking at her through narrowed eyes.

Kate gave him a long cold look, then with what she hoped was assured dignity she turned away from him and continued slowly to walk up the stairs. That dignity wavered when she realised that Charles was following her, slowly, steadily. As she reached the corner where the stair turned under the high window she sensed that the gap between them was closing, and involuntarily she quickened her pace.

Below them, Madeau, coming from the kitchen, paused, looking up in surprise before with a smile on her face she went on in the direction of the dining room. Kate felt her heart begin to pound and she darted a quick nervous glance over her shoulder, then abandoning all pretence she made a wild dash for her room.

Inside, she lay back against the solid wooden door with a sense of relief, but almost at once she felt the handle turn beneath her fingers, the pressure of his weight as he leaned against it. Desperately she pushed her toe into the crack where the wood joined the carpet, but any hope she might have had of that as a security was abandoned as she saw her foot slide inch by inch as the door was forced open.

Damn, she thought. Damn! Why do people make bedrooms without properly locking doors? Then she had the inspiration. The bathroom door had a lock, and with a bound she had crossed the room, throwing herself inside the bathroom, sliding the bolt firmly into place with a click.

'Kate!' Charles was rattling the door impatiently. 'Don't behave like a child. Surely we can talk about this sensibly?'

'We can talk downstairs.'

'I prefer to discuss the matter now.'

'Not in my bedroom.'

She stood, her cheek pressed to the smooth white surface of the door, listening intently, and heard the wearied sigh, then the sound of his feet retreating across the room. But instead of going to the door she knew that he stood in the middle of the floor, probably glaring at the locked door with that exasperated frown she was beginning to know so well.

Struck by the sheer farce of the situation, she allowed a tiny giggle to escape her lips and reached for one of the soft towels to wipe the tear which unexpectedly slid down her cheek. Then, suspecting some activity from the bedroom she applied her cheek again to the door. To her indignation, instead of the reassuring click of the outer door, she heard the doors of her cupboards being pulled open and the faint rattle of coathangers being pushed along the rails.

'Charles!' She beat on the door panels with closed fists quite as if she were a prisoner.

'*Oui, chérie?*' His tone was as mild as milk but irritatingly preoccupied.

'What are you doing in my cupboard?'

'What did you say, Kate?' He walked to the bathroom door and tried the knob.

'Don't do that!' To emphasise the point she banged with her fist on the door. 'Weren't you ever told not to intrude on a lady in the bathroom?'

'You're not a lady, Kate. You're my wife.'

'Well, *your* wife couldn't possibly be both. That's true enough. Anyway, old jokes like that deserve to be decently buried.'

She waited for a reply, but when none came she was perversely disappointed to be deprived of the stimulation of their brief repartee. Again she banged at the door. 'Charles!' She leaned her forehead against it, straining for a sound. 'Charles!' She banged again, but this time disappointed, a spoilt child.

Slowly, watching herself in the mirror over the washbasin, she washed her hands under the running tap, then dried them on the towel. She shook her head at her image, regretful now that she had presented such a picture to Françoise. If only Charles had asked her nicely . . . She went to the door, then listening carefully to the total silence she slid back the bolt, opened it the merest chink, one eye to the crack showing that the coast was clear, the outer door firmly shut. Half in relief, wholly disappointed, she stepped out into the bedroom.

'Now, Kate.' Looking neither amused nor angry, Charles got up from the small upholstered chair by the open window and looked down at her, having carefully positioned himself so that it was impossible for her to retreat again into the bathroom. 'I'm glad you decided to come out.'

'Only because I thought you'd gone,' she stated

coldly. 'I haven't changed my mind. I don't usually entertain men in my bedroom and I would be grateful if you would leave.'

'Very right and proper, my dear Kate. And I'm very glad that you've reassured me. But I think in this case we can make an exception. As I told you that first night,' he surveyed her condescendingly, 'you are in absolutely no danger from me.'

'You could have fooled me.' Her voice was tart and she cursed herself when she saw the faint smile cross his face.

'I think, my Kate,' his voice slow and deep, infinitely beguiling so that she felt a betraying tremor at the base of her spine, 'that perhaps we are trying, not exactly succeeding, but trying to fool each other.'

Kate swallowed hard, staring up at him coldly, determined not to betray by so much as a flicker of eyelashes the effect he was having on her. 'I don't understand what you mean. But I would like to know what you were doing in my cupboard.' She wrenched her eyes from his, searching round the room for some clue. And she didn't have far to look, for there, tossed casually down in a pile in one corner, were jeans and blouses, all those things she had been wearing for the past few days as part of her plan.

'How dare you!' The long lashes swept up, the blue eyes flashed with an icy rage. 'How dare you come into my room and rummage about! That is contemptible!'

'You have a cupboard full of what at first glance seem to be rather attractive dresses and I refuse to tolerate you going about looking exactly like a beatnik—and a scruffy beatnik at that.'

'I shall go about exactly as I like!'

'Not in my house.' Now his voice was hard and uncompromising. 'In this one place my wishes are supreme. You have made your point as far as I am concerned. I understand that you want to wear a hair shirt until Antoine comes to claim you.' His arrogant condescension made her gorge rise. 'Although,' and he gave a short sneering laugh, 'you might find the hair shirt more appropriate when you return to the château.'

'How can you?' Her voice trembled with her emotion, again tears trembled on her lashes. 'You speak as if Antoine . . .'

'What do you know of Antoine? You really think you *know* each other? I tell you, Kate,' now he stepped forward and took both her wrists in his hands, circling round them with his fingers as if he would make her his prisoner, 'you will be tired of Antoine in six months.'

'I thought you loved him,' she protested. 'Like a brother, you said.'

'I do love him like a brother. That does not mean I can't recognise his faults.'

'I suppose you have none!'

'Even I have a few.' He grinned with a sudden change of mood. 'But they are different ones from Antoine's.' The smile faded, leaving him watchful, quiet, even a little grim. 'He is not the man to satisfy you, Kate.'

'Whereas you are, I suppose.' The words burst impulsively from her lips and the instant they were spoken she would have snatched them back. They stared at each other, she imagined that the dark eyes darkened. Charles's lips were tight, stretched over his teeth as he answered her.

'Why did you say that, Kate? I wonder.' Abruptly he relinquished his grip on her wrists. 'Especially when

I have told you more than once just how very safe you
are.'

Kate turned away, rubbing her wrists as if they hurt,
biting her lip with vexation. Then when she felt his
hands on her shoulders she shuddered, only just resist-
ing the impulse to lie back against him, to encourage
the comfort she knew would come if his hands slipped
down her body, turning her towards him.

But his fingers had no tenderness, they were hard and
cruel, biting into the tender skin under the thin material
of her blouse. And his voice was hard, determined to
dominate. 'Give me those things you're wearing, Kate.
I can add them to the pile and Georges can put them
on a bonfire.'

'You really are the most patronising man . . .'
Snatched from her yearning tenderness, Kate wrenched
herself from his grip and turned to face him with a
stormy resentful expression.

'Am I, Kate?' he asked almost mildly, and the sus-
picion that he was laughing at her only increased her
aggravation.

'. . . And there is no way . . .'

'Yes, there is a way, Kate. And I am quite capable of
taking it. If you refuse to be sensible.'

'What do you mean?'

'I mean, my dear,' now he made no attempt to conceal the pleasure he was finding in their contest, 'that I
am quite capable of removing them myself. If you fail
to see things my way.'

'You wouldn't dare!' Her words were braver than
her emotions. Especially when he lounged, one hand
looped round the open bathroom door, smiling down at
her with that mocking, heart-stopping look in his eyes

that should be such a warning.

'I would, Kate.' Although he spoke softly she knew that it was no idle boast he made.

'I'd shout for Madeau.' Nervously her fingers closed over the open collar of her blouse.

He shrugged. 'She would never hear. And if she did she would smile indulgently and think that perhaps we were enjoying ourselves in the most natural way possible.'

'Why is it,' Kate tried to ignore the throbbing of her own heart, tried to stare as if she were completely unmoved by the sight of his tall lithe figure, 'that your mind always seems to come back to one thing? Anyway, Madeau must know that we don't share a bedroom and . . .'

'Ah, but I'm taking particular care that she suspects nothing like that. Put it down to my masculine pride if you like, Kate. No man really likes his staff to think that his bride of a few days is content to spend her nights alone. I assure you that my gallery bedroom is completely . . . virginal, if I can use that word . . . by the time Madeau comes in at seven-thirty in the mornings.'

Kate stared up at him, unwilling to admit that before she left her room in the mornings she thumped the pillow on the other side of the bed, tossed the bedclothes as if a man had been sleeping there. Not for the world would she have liked him to know that she too wanted Madeau to think that the bridegroom found the bride desirable.

For a long moment Charles looked down at her, watching the emotions chase over her features. Then in a sort of lazy swoop, his hands reached out again for her shoulders, causing her to gasp nervously.

'Kate, Kate.' Lightly he shook her. 'Why are you so afraid? I have told you, have I not . . .' He sighed suddenly, as suddenly releasing her. 'Shall we call it quits, Kate? Much as I enjoy our little spats I think for the time being we must forgo that pleasure. All I'm asking now is for you to do as I want in this one thing. Will you, Kate?'

'All right.' She had not intended to agree with him, to give in so easily to his masculine power.

'Good girl!' He leaned forward, allowing his lips to brush gently against her cheek, his hand to touch the neck of her blouse. 'I don't know whether to be pleased or sorry, Kate.' Then with a sardonic smile he turned and the door closed behind him.

She stood staring, unable to bear the explosion of pain in her chest. Oh God, what was happening to her? Trembling hands were pressed to her eyes, then with a groan she ran over to the bed and lay face down on the cover, rubbing her forehead distractedly over the roughness of the lace.

I love Antoine! Desperately she tried to recall the perfection of those idyllic days in London when they had fallen in love, to bring his image to her mind. But his features seemed distractingly elusive, slipping out of her memory each time she thought they had been captured. And always they were replaced by those that were disquietening in their familiarity, stronger, fiercer, lacking most of that gentleness which she had first loved. But now she was afraid, terribly afraid that now she had known the second cousin, the first would never do.

CHAPTER SEVEN

THE next day Kate and Charles went into town together to buy the food that they decided would be
necessary for the party the following day. Kate was
pleased that she was obliged to wear one of her pretty
dresses, and although Charles said nothing when she
slipped into the dining-room his eyes gave her the message of approval as he wished her good morning.

Madeau was less reticent when she and Kate sat at
the large kitchen table poring over the long list of
things that were required from the shops. 'Your dress
is so pretty, *madame*.' Kate knew that she was being
encouraged to give up her previous bad habits, and
strangely didn't mind all that much.

'Yes, it is a nice dress. I bought it in a sale before I
came over.' She rose and did a little twirl so that
Madeau could see how the skirt flared out from the hip
seam, then smoothed the long bodice where it clung to
her figure. She caught sight of herself in the mirror and
momentarily wished that she had done something about
her hair, but some perversity had stopped her. She
wasn't going to capitulate completely and perhaps give
Charles the idea that she was too eager to do exactly
what he wanted.

Just as last night she had compromised. She had
given her word to abandon jeans and blouses, but that

didn't mean that slacks suits were out completely. So she had worn a pair of harem trousers, silky white lamé, perfect with the high-heeled sandals in pink, their straps drawing attention to her slender ankles. The top was a loose blouson style, the slashed low neckline assuring anyone who was interested that she wore nothing underneath.

Somewhat to her disappointment Charles had made no comment, although he had hardly taken his eyes from her as they sat opposite each other at the round table. Though she had noticed that he had filled his wine-glass a little more often than he usually did and that possibly had had the effect of making him silent and withdrawn. It had almost been a relief, a disappointment too, of course, but a relief when after dinner he had excused himself saying that he had better go and ring round all the people he wanted to invite to the party.

But this morning he did seem less tense. And so, decided Kate with a last satisfied look at her reflection in the brilliant turquoise dress, did she. She smiled at Madeau in an excess of pleasure and excitement as she picked up the handwritten list from the table.

'Is this all, then, Madeau?' She pored over her own cramped handwriting.

'I think it is.'

'Then I had better go before my master begins to feel impatient.'

'I'm glad to see that you're getting your priorities right at last.' The laconic voice from the door made Kate turn round in surprise, but she was able to laugh ruefully, although something about his expression brought the colour into her cheeks. 'Ready?' He turned back towards the hall.

'Almost.' She followed him, then began to run up-stairs taking two steps at a time.

'Hurry.' His eyes followed until she was out of sight and she ran, filled with breathless excitement, into her bedroom.

She sang faintly under her breath as she tied the blue and white scarf round her head, knotting it under her hair at the nape of her neck. Then with a final touch of lipstick to her already pink mouth, she turned, picked up her bag from the foot of the bed and, still humming, ran back down to the empty hall. She paused at the foot of the stairs, arrested for a moment by the strange sound that was on her lips. It seemed a whole lifetime since she had felt the urge to sing—and now she was actually happy.

Thoughtfully, she walked out to where Charles was waiting by the car. He stood still, watching her walk towards him over the cobbles, making her as conscious of herself as she was of him. When she reached him she felt breathless, stood looking up at him, both hidden behind their dark glasses but each intensely searching for something, she had no idea what. Above, the soft cooing of the doves was seductive.

Then he smiled. The dark planes of his face softened, lines round the slanting eyes crinkled, the teeth shone dazzling in the bright morning's sun. 'Ready?' The word that had been brief and somehow critical indoors was now like a caress.

'Ready.' On her lips it was a breathless, yielding statement, and as she folded her skirt beneath her to slip past the door he held for her she felt ridiculously, foolishly happy.

. They spent two hours happily searching out the food which Madeau had ordered, Kate frowning over the list she held, striking through words with satisfaction when they found exactly what was required. But all the time Kate kept exclaiming over the charm of the little town which she confessed to Charles she had never even heard of before.

'Sarlat-Le-Canèda.' She rolled the name round her mouth as they sat under a wide umbrella in the pavement café where they were drinking iced coffee from long frosted glasses. 'It's such an unusual name. And such a beautiful town.' She waved an arm towards the mediaeval houses opposite with their overhanging upper storeys and tiny lead-paned windows. 'Some of those old courtyards . . . they're just out of this world!'

'Yes.' He drew deeply on the long black cheroot, then blew the smoke slowly away from her. 'It is all very charming.' His voice had become very French, quite different in her ears from the perfect, almost accentless English that he usually spoke. His mouth was relaxed and smiling so that she could hardly take her eyes from it.

'So,' at last she was able to speak and tried to adopt a matter-of-fact, almost chatty tone. 'I would think you must be terribly happy here, Charles. Now that you've settled, I mean. It's so much nicer than . . .' She hesitated, wondering if what she were saying would be painful for him to hear.

'You mean . . .' The cigar moved to his mouth again, his eyes crinkled against the faintly acrid smoke. '. . . You mean that you prefer it to the Auvergne, Kate.'

'Of course. I love it here.' She stretched back in her

chair, clasping her hands behind her head. 'And your home is so much more comfortable than the château. The thought of living in such a place . . .' She sat up, shivering a little in spite of the warm sunshine, and stealing a careful glance to see if her words had had any reaction. Then as there was no answer to her original question, rather more tentatively, 'You do like it, don't you, Charles?'

'Of course I like it. As I told you, I've seen it take shape, I've been in on every step of its development, from a group of tumbledown buildings into what most people would think was a comfortable and rather desirable house.' He was speaking so lightly that she wondered if he was determined to avoid answering. 'But as to home, Kate—it takes more than a pleasant situation and elegant furniture. Besides,' his movement towards the packages which had been placed on a spare chair indicated that he was no longer willing to be interrogated on the matter, 'I'm away from here such a lot. I seem to spend more time on planes than I do in La Pigeonnière.' And with the raising of one finger he summoned a waiter and the bill.

Nevertheless there was something intimate about the situation that Kate cherished. It was, as she reminded herself, a memory that would have to last a long time but one to be savoured at the moment. So as they wandered through the market, piled high with the rich produce of the surrounding countryside, she made no attempt to hide the pleasure that she was experiencing. And Charles seemed willing enough to respond. It was, she thought rather sadly, almost the first time they had been completely natural with each other. And if only . . .

'Shall we take these things back to the car?' Charles, now piled high with parcels which threatened to tumble from his arms, appealed to her as if she were totally mistress of his fate. 'I'm beginning to feel like one of those hen-pecked husbands whose dominating wives have bought up the store.'

Kate laughed, throwing back her head in amusement at the picture he had portrayed. 'I just can't see you in that role, Charles.'

'No?' One black eyebrow crooked wickedly. 'Not even now?'

'Not even now,' she assured him. 'In fact I have a sneaking feeling that you're enjoying yourself.'

'Do you?' he grinned, refusing to confirm or deny. 'Anyway, let's find the car, then when you've checked the list I'll take you for lunch.'

'Won't Madeau expect us?'

'No. I told her we wouldn't be back till late. We can drive back along the river. I want you to see something of the country while you're here.'

Even the reminder that she was merely a bird of passage could do little to spoil Kate's enjoyment of the day. They found their way to a small restaurant just off the main square, tucked away in one of the charming courtyards she had remarked upon and where the tables spilled out from the building to a small raised garden at the side.

'Where would you like to sit?' They stood in the dim interior, while the *patron*, who gave every appearance of being pleased to see Charles, hovered beside them. Kate looked quickly round the room, noticing that the only free table was squeezed up against the wall by the kitchen door, then her eyes moved longingly to the pink-covered tables in the garden.

'Oh, Charles,' without thinking what she was doing she slipped her hand into his, 'would you mind sitting outside?' The dark look he turned on her made her remember what she was about and hurriedly she withdrew her hand and he made no attempt to stop her. 'It looks . . . it looks so cool under the trees,' she stammered.

And it was. They sat listening to the faint sound that the wind made as it stirred the listless leaves, hearing insects drone round the flowers that cascaded down the high mossy wall at the back of the garden. Only three of the tables were occupied, and it was pleasant to think that they were in a secluded, private place, even if they had little that was private to say to each other.

'Thank you for bringing me here.' It was Kate who broke the silence which had had nothing awkward about it.

'It was my pleasure.' His tone was lazy, faintly teasing, giving her courage to continue the game.

'Do you come here often?' She leaned her elbows on the table, cupping her chin in her hands.

'Not often.' He imitated her attitude, bringing his face very close to hers. 'Only when I have the chance of bringing a beautiful model out to lunch.'

'I'm sure,' she smiled into his eyes, 'that you have the opportunity very often. Now what about the gorgeous Auriol?'

'What about her?' he teased. 'Are you asking if I think your description is accurate? It is, *chérie*. She is gorgeous.'

'Oh . . .!' she pouted.

'You know, I'm beginning to think . . .' his hand

came out, hovering about her face, then resting gently on her bare arm, '. . . that perhaps you are just a little bit jealous.'

'Are you?' Her eyes narrowed as her enjoyment of the game increased. 'And what of Françoise, is she too jealous?'

'I don't know. But she needn't be.' Kate withdrew from his touch and was annoyed to see him put back his head and laugh. 'And you needn't be either, my sweet.'

Before Kate had the chance to protest that of course she wasn't jealous, the waiter came forward with long menus and the next few minutes were taken up discussing what they would eat. There was a fairly long discussion between the two men which ended when Charles raised an eyebrow in her direction.

'Shall I choose for you, Kate?'

'Yes.' Happily she relinquished the menu, reflecting that he was the kind of man who would always want to decide things for you. Whereas Antoine . . . A tiny cloud darkened her spirits. She had the feeling that he would always give in. To his mother—and his wife.

'You really must begin to learn French, Kate.' The waiter had gone and Charles was leaning back in his seat now, seeming to take a long view of her. 'Antoine will expect it.' It was as if their minds had been in communication.

'Then Antoine must find out that he doesn't always get what he wants!' Kate turned away, regretting whatever interruption had brought an end to their mood of childish escapism.

'Poor Antoine.' Charles seemed to express genuine regret, but before Kate had time to ask angrily what he meant the waiter had returned with a bottle which he showed, received a brief nod of approval and then by the time he had filled their glasses, another waiter was wheeling a trolley up to their table.

'*Madame?*' The boy was very young and inexperienced and the eyes he turned on Kate were blatantly admiring. '*Fruits de mer?*'

'Yes—*oui. Merci.*' The smile with which she responded caused him to drop his spoon on to the path and he blushed as he picked it up and put it out of the way on the lower shelf.

'*Monsieur?*' Charles, who had been watching the scene with a faintly cynical smile, nodded, then smiled at Kate as he raised his knife and fork to begin on the seafood crêpe.

'Perhaps I was wrong the other night. Obviously there are dangers in taking your sunglasses off! You like it?' He indicated her plate, diverting the conversation from the personal.

'It's absolutely delicious.' Kate ate with relish. 'But then I seem to say that whenever I eat in France. You obviously have the reputation you deserve.'

'Well, of course things aren't as good as they were. Too many tourists these days. But . . .'

'But I imagine . . . they say the very same thing in New York when all the planes disgorge their loads of Europeans.'

'Maybe they do,' he smiled. 'Anyway, this seafood isn't exactly a regional dish, but the next one definitely is. Ah, here it comes.' He looked up as the waiter returned carrying a huge silver dish and began serving what looked like portions of duck, with tiny potatoes and green peas.

When they were alone Charles watched as Kate cut through the crisp brown skin, into the succulent moist flesh, smiled as he saw her munch with obvious enjoyment.

'It's *confit de canard*, I'm glad you like it. You can find it in lots of other parts of the country, but I think it tastes best on its home ground. Now tell me,' with the typical change of topic which she found disconcerting, he put down his fork and looked intently at her, 'you spoke of writing letters. I hope you have been in contact with your mother.'

Kate tried to subdue the wave of guilt that threatened to overwhelm her and felt pleased that she was able to look at him with a cool level gaze. 'No. I did tell you that I wasn't sure when she and Andrew would be back in New York, so there seemed little point in writing just so that the letter would be lying for weeks on the mat in their flat.'

'Don't you think, Kate, that you should forget how upset you were when your mother married and . . .'

'I didn't say I was upset. I don't know why you should jump to such conclusions, I . . .'

'Of course you were upset. I'm not blaming you. All I'm saying is that because you've been hurt you ought not to . . .'

'You, Charles, are the last person to give such advice.' Carefully Kate wiped her mouth with the pink linen napkin, wondering why her appetite should have gone so quickly. 'You've waited a long time to get back at your aunt, so you if anyone should understand. Besides,' she picked up her fork and knife and began to push the joint round her plate, 'you're wrong in your assumption. I had no intention of exacting some kind of petty revenge on my mother and Andrew.' Even as she spoke she knew this was not entirely true and a faint increase in colour stained her cheeks. 'I suppose,' she smiled across the table, shrugging with a trace of self-mockery, 'my problem is that when I was young I fell madly in love with Young Lochinvar. You know the poem . . .'

'You mean,' the dark eyes were so intense in their speculation that Kate felt the blood throb dangerously in her veins, 'the one who came out of the west?'

'What?' Her face was suddenly pale, she looked at him with a wide bewildered stare.

'Young Lochinvar, *chérie*.' His voice was low and tender, his hand reached across the table to caress hers. 'The one you fell in love with.'

'Oh yes.' Kate blinked and looked down at the dark fingers curving round hers, the thumb moving slowly back and forth across her wrist. Her heart felt as if it would burst with the emotion she felt, a mixture of all the bitter-sweet feelings she had ever known. She longed to weep and even as she thought of it, she saw a tear drop on to the back of his hand, shimmer like crystal for an instant on the dark hair and then disappear. 'As I said, I fell in love with Young Lochinvar when I was about eight, and since then I suppose I've always had this romantic notion about an elopement.' She looked up at him, her eyes wide and brilliant with unshed tears. 'Please don't dash all my childhood dreams, Charles.'

'That I would hate to do.' To her dismay he withdrew his hand, leaving her deprived and alone. 'You have had enough to eat?'

'Yes. I truly enjoyed it.' She looked at the only half-eaten meal and then at his plate. 'It's a pity that neither of us was hungry.'

She refused anything else and after they had had coffee they walked back to the parking place in the main square where they had left the car under the shade of some trees. Neither of them spoke as Charles negotiated the car through the narrow streets of the town, still busy with tourists and shoppers despite the heat of the afternoon, then out along the route to Les Eyzies.

They swished gently along the quiet roads, relieved to be out of the town and traffic, each busy with thoughts engendered by their exchange in the restaurant. The windows of the car were open as they drove and Kate pulled the scarf from her head, allowing the soft warmth of the breeze to blow through her hair while reflecting that when she got home she would wash out the oil for the last time. It was too late now to be bothered about curbing . . . Hastily she forced her mind away from a topic that was becoming all too obsessive, instead lying back in her seat, her eyes firmly closed, trying to concentrate on the sweet music from the radio that washed about her.

But she opened them when a few moments later she felt the car veer off the main road and drive along a rutted track at a much reduced pace. Questioningly she turned to Charles, who cast a quick tight smile in her direction.

'I thought you were going to sleep.' Then reapplying his attention to the narrow tree-lined path as it meandered over some undulating fields, he stabbed a finger towards where she could see their route opening out on to a grassy meadow. 'We're almost at the river. I wondered if you would like to sit there for a bit. It's cool and shady. We can watch the boats passing.'

'Sounds nice.' She yawned with just a shade of ostentation. 'I can't think of anything better on such a hot afternoon than a sleep on a river bank.'

'I didn't say you were to sleep.' He pulled in at the side of the track and turned to her with a grin. 'I expect you to entertain me.'

Kate tried to smile back, but quickly looked away from him and reached into the rear seat for the rug which was always kept folded there.

'Do you want me to bring the rug?'

'Of course.' Charles got out of the car, but his eyes followed her with sardonic understanding as she stepped out and began to smooth, then retie her hair in the scarf and reach for her handbag. 'Give me that.' He took the rug from her arm, brushing against her with his fingers.

Kate followed him, seeing hardly anything of the luxuriant green of the vegetation, conscious only of his tall figure, the wide shoulders under the immaculately fitting linen jacket, then as he spread out the tartan blanket, he turned round to face her. He said nothing, but there was a half-smile on his face as he looked at her, as if, thought Kate with terrifying certainty, he understood something of the fears and doubts that were threatening to overwhelm her reason.

She saw him remove his jacket and toss it down on the grass, then, searching her face, he pulled at the dark silk tie. 'You don't mind, I hope, Kate?' There was laughter in his voice as if he knew the effect that dark throat, that wide expanse of chest had on her pulses and emotions. With an effort she wrenched her eyes from the fingers that slowly undid the buttons of his shirt, threw her handbag on to the ground and sank down beside it.

'Mind?' She pretended not to understand the question and kept her eyes fixed on the swift silent flow of the dark green water a few yards from them. 'Mind what?'

But he seemed to have forgotten their conversation, for he dropped down on the rug beside her, supporting himself on one elbow so that his head was on a level with hers. Resolutely Kate kept her face averted, although she knew that he was studying her profile with mocking intensity. Wondering if she would ever be able to hide the devastating intensity of her feelings, she pointed out to the other side of the bank. 'What's that building?'

Lazily he moved his head, following the direction she was pointing, and it was a moment before he answered.

'I suspect, Kate, I don't know for certain, but I very much suspect that it's a cowshed.'

Kate turned to glare at him, but quite suddenly he had lain back on the rug with his eyes closed, a piece of grass between his lips. Rejecting a sudden gush of tears, she looked again at the field on the opposite bank, seeing clearly for the first time what she had pointed to. In the middle of the lush meadow, surrounded by those burnt cream cows with the gentle eyes, bells round their necks chiming softly as they munched, was a small stone building that could be nothing other than a cowshed. What a fool she was! She dashed her hand across her eyes and looked down at the recumbent figure by her side. The broad chest was rising and falling regularly as if even now he was dropping into sleep. She longed to slip her hand inside the shirt, to move her fingers over the warmth of his skin, but she knew that to do so would be fatal. Some sense told her that no matter how close Charles was to sleep she would find her hand imprisoned, she would be forced back on to the rug and he would be looking down at her, dominating her. And he would imagine that she was encouraging him to . . . To what? she wondered, and blushed when the answer she would rather have avoided slipped into her mind.

She sighed and lay down, looking up at the tiny patches of blue that forced themselves through the thick canopy of leaves above them. And she moved to the edge of the blanket in an effort to escape the influence that even his sleeping form seemed capable of exerting so powerfully.

Eventually she got up, first walking with care silently over the thick grass so that she would not disturb him, then going with swift sure steps towards the river, gazing down at it with moody apprehension. She sighed, reached for a blade of grass, stuck it, as Charles had done, between her teeth, and began to stroll along the bank.

Fields stretched down from the road towards the river, some divided by fences, some by ditches and rough clumps of hedging but all of them rich with ripe wheat and ready to be cut. Kate hardly noticed them. She was too obsessed with her own thoughts, too conscious of the truth of all that Charles had said to her at lunch.

What mad folly could have persuaded her to embark on such a course? She shuddered, thinking of what awful plight she might have fallen into. Madame Savoney-Morlet struck her as the kind of slightly deranged woman who would go to almost any lengths to get her own way. And if Charles hadn't made such an opportune offer who knew what kind of plan she might have concocted to ensure that Kate and Antoine did not marry! Oh God! Kate put her hand to her head, then realising that the river bank had narrowed to almost nothing she turned to retrace her step.

The sun, although it was now late afternoon, was still hot and the field on her left was bathed in a shimmer of golden light. At last the sheer beauty, the tranquillity of it, like some old Impressionist picture, forced itself into her consciousness. She paused, leaning her back against a tree, grateful for the shade and a moment to escape from her own pervasive worries.

The field was sprinkled with patches of red where poppies had invaded the crop, making vivid contrast with the wheat while down the side of the field, stunted twisted hawthorn trees marked the boundary, diminishing in the hazy mist as they wandered towards the horizon. Unconscious fingers reached for one of the silky blobs of red, only the sticky feel of juice on her fingers drawing her attention to what she was doing.

She looked down at the softness already drooping in her hands, then touched the full flower, wondering at the perfection of the splash of black in its heart at the frill of pollen-laden stamens. Her finger raised the half-open bud, vaguely regretful that her unthinking action had deprived it of life. Then a sudden click brought her startled eyes up and she saw Charles coming towards her turning the spool of his camera.

'Girl with poppy,' he explained as he came closer. Then, 'I wondered where you had gone.'

Kate turned abruptly from him, scarcely trusting

herself to reply, her eyes looking far over the field.
'Isn't this the most beautiful spot you ever saw?' The
wildness she felt was hidden in her voice. 'It reminds
me of a picture I saw once—Monet, I think—with a
girl walking through a field. And there were poppies ...'
She faltered, leaned back against the trunk of the tree,
turning to him with a feeling of hopeless longing.

'Do you like butter?' Facing her, he leaned against
the tree, supported by one hand somewhere above her
right shoulder, and he was smiling down into her face.
Something he was twirling in his right hand attracted
her attention and she saw that he was holding a butter-
cup under her raised chin.

'Do you like butter? My Kate.'

Kate shook her head as if such a futile gesture however negative could protect her from the irresistible
force of her own desires, from the white fire that was
racing through her veins, consuming her. Her eyes
moved giddily from his, to his mouth hovering so close
to her own, then her head drooped so that the dark
chest, the dark silky hair beneath the thin shirt, were
so near that by sinking just a little against the trunk she
could have pressed her lips to that throbbing pulse of
his throat.

But before she could do that his arm had moved
strongly round her waist, supporting her, drawing her
closely against him. Startled, fearful, her eyes flicked
wide to look at him, and what she saw in his face made
her hold her breath.

'Kate.' It was a husky whisper now and his hand
slipped lower, moulding her body against him with a
fierce possessiveness which thrilled yet caused her to
tremble with fear. 'Kate,' he said again with a kind of

lingering, amused despair, and his mouth closed on hers.

Just for a moment she would abandon herself to the bewildering, overpowering sweetness, to the gentle fierce exploration of her mouth. Then when she knew that the moment was over, when warning signals were jangling in her mind, a hand on the nape of her neck imprisoned her, holding her immovably linked to him.

Another moment's bliss; Kate, obeying some instinctive urge, slipped both hands inside his shirt, moving over the warm satin softness of his chest, her fingers touching the dark curling hair in a caress. The groan that she drew from his lips made her pulses race uncontrolled and she leaned her head back as his mouth moved to her throat and lower to the deeply plunging neckline of her dress.

There was no resistance in her as she felt his hand reach for the zip at the back of her dress, then his mouth was searching for the firm sweet swell of her breast, while a tumult of response burned through her. Again he sought her lips, demanding a submission she was willing to show, heart throbbed against heart, Charles moved his body gently against hers so that she felt the faint roughness score her breasts.

She knew now that nothing she had experienced with Antoine had been like this. She linked her hands round Charles's neck, felt his answering power as he strained her form against his. Poor Antoine!

She had no idea that his name had escaped her lips till she was thrust aside and Charles's eyes were blazing down at her with a fury she could not understand, his teeth bared in a threatening gash.

'Antoine! Did you call his name when I was making love to you?'

'No . . . I . . .' Deprived of the support of his arms, she lay back, half fainting, against the tree. 'Charles . . .' Her voice was a sob and she held out her hands appealingly.

Now the eyes that had been so passionate a moment before were consumed with fury, the mouth that had been so tormenting was a thin hard line.

'No, damn it!' He let out the words as if he hated her. 'I refuse to be a surrogate lover for anyone. Not even for Antoine would I adopt such a rôle.' His eyes travelled coldly contemptuous over her dishevelled appearance, over her heaving bosom. 'I suggest we meet back at the car in a few minutes. We'll try to forget this sordid episode ever happened.' And the next moment he was striding away from her, the camera he had been using lying on a tree stump, as despised and forgotten as she was herself.

CHAPTER EIGHT

THE return journey to the house was completed in an atmosphere of total silence, Kate sitting hunched in her seat, gazing out of the side window, trying to avoid looking at the dark intimidating man by her side. He drove with a kind of repressed fury that showed itself in the way the car cornered with a screeching of tyres and a wild scattering of pebbles as they accelerated along unmade roads.

At last they drove into the courtyard of La Pigeon-nière, and as he switched off the engine Kate ventured a glance in his direction. His profile was as if carved in marble and not by a softening of any gesture did he give an indication that his fury was abating. At last he spoke, and it was without looking at her, his manner as cold as ice.

'I shall take the things in to the kitchen. Madeau will put them away later. You must be tired, so perhaps you would like to go upstairs to your bedroom.'

Anger surged inside Kate at the insulting way he spoke as well as his assumption that she could be hidden away in her room. Even if it was true that she longed for nothing so much as to bury her head in her pillow and cry, not for the world would she have confessed as much to him. So, not trusting herself to reply, she got out of the car, slamming the door as the only way of showing what she felt.

Ignoring what he had said, she picked up one basket of groceries, walked into the kitchen and put it on the table, then returned to the hall. She had reached the stair when Charles shouldered the door open, heavily laden with packages, but he paused when he saw her, his eyes resting impassively on her turbulent face.

'Oh, I may have to go out this evening. I hope you won't mind eating alone. Madeau will make you something.'

'Thank you.' Her voice matched his for iciness. 'I'm quite capable of making a meal for myself should I want anything. Might I ask where you're going?' She paused significantly. 'Or would that be tactless?'

'What is that supposed to mean?' Charles's eyes narrowed dangerously, making her regret such a cheap remark, but she refused to let him know that she was in any way intimidated.

'Oh, I merely thought that you might be going to see Françoise. I know she'll be very . . . understanding when you explain just how things are at home. I'm sure she'll have no scruples about being a surrogate—wasn't that the word you used?' With admirable control Kate was able to assume a faint smile. 'In fact where you're concerned she would, I think, welcome the opportunity.' Then collecting the remnants of her tattered dignity about her she walked unhurriedly up to her room.

Only there did all her self-control desert her so that she threw herself on to the bed in a noisy storm of weeping that went on till she lay utterly exhausted, staring at the net curtains as they moved gently at the open window. Several times she thought she heard a sound in the corridor outside and held her breath, listening with a desperate urgent longing for something that would indicate that Charles had come to make peace with her. But all she heard as she lay there was the hammering of her own heart and the vague creaks and groans of an old house, cooling as the sun moved round in the sky.

It was a long time before hope faded altogether, but when it did, Kate dragged herself from the bed and walked over to a mirror where she could study her reflection. Vaguely she pondered on the girl who had gone out and the one who had come back. Was it possible they could be the same person—the first so fresh, bursting with life and excitement, this one with the sunken red-rimmed eyes, the distraught haunted expression. The first borne on an expectant wave of love, the second cast aside by a brutal rejection.

There, she had admitted it at last. It was love. This burning fiery ecstasy and despair, this stormy passionate longing could be nothing else but love. And it was all to do with Charles, nothing with Antoine.

Had she really spoken his name when the final knowledge came to her? She could only assume she had. And that brief fleeting moment of sympathy for him, that vague regret for those carefree tender days in London had saved her. Her hand curved over the breast where his lips had begun their passionate trembling onslaught. Saved her? Bleakly she regarded herself, trying to ignore her own burning unsatisfied body, before with a despairing cry she turned away from the mirror. There was nothing to be gained by self-deceit. She knew that she would regret to the end of her life that accident which had made Charles recoil from her. She would regret it for ever, knowing that she would never have another opportunity.

Kate walked to the bathroom and began taking off her clothes. A moment later she was standing under the shower wishing she could find some recipe for relieving the pain inside her as surely as warm water could ease the body's aches. Half an hour later she was slipping naked between the clean, sweet-smelling cotton sheets. It seemed impossible even to hope for sleep, but a few moments later her breathing deepened, lengthened and she drifted away from her tormented life to blissful oblivion.

It was evening when she woke and she lay for a long time watching the shadows in her room lengthen, the last golden streaks fade from the sky before, regretfully, she forced herself from the warm cocoon. She dressed quickly, hardly noticing what she was wearing, and ran downstairs, her heart hammering against her ribs. A door somewhere opened and Kate felt a blow of disappointment when she heard Madeau's faintly concerned voice behind her.

'*Madame?* You are all right?'

'Of course, Madeau.' Kate stretched ostentatiously. 'I had such a wonderful sleep.'

'Ah. Monsieur Charles said you were sleeping so peacefully, he could not disturb you.'

'Charles said so . . .?' Deliberately hiding her face, Kate turned away, adjusting some of the flowers she had arranged the previous day in a shining yellow bowl. 'When was that, Madeau?'

'Oh, more than an hour ago. I wanted to know about your meal. He told me that he was going out, so I asked him to go up and find out when you would be . . .'

'But didn't he tell you,' Kate's voice was brittle as she turned to face the other woman, 'that I would get something for myself? I told him that earlier.'

'Yes, he did say so, *madame*.'

'Then I suggest that you go across to the flat, Madeau.' She smiled in what she hoped was a relaxed manner. 'We had a lovely lunch and I'll just make myself an omelette. I might even take it out and eat it beside the pool. You can have a rest tonight.'

'Are you certain, *madame*?'

'Positive.' She went over and draped an arm about Madeau's shoulders. 'After all, you shouldn't be doing too much. I mean to see to it . . . that you take life more easily.' She felt guilty as she spoke, for of course she would be in no position to influence any such thing.

'Very well, *madame*. *Merci*.'

'But before you go, Madeau, tell me what I can do for tomorrow. Can I prepare any of the food?'

'Ah no, *madame*. Monsieur Charles ordered meat to be delivered and it is already cooked for the *boeuf en gêlée*. Tomorrow we shall be busy with salads and desserts; there are all those delicious cheeses you brought from Sarlat and Monsieur Charles has ordered strawberries to be delivered. Besides, my sister will be here to help. And Georges will be with us in the evening to assist with the drinks. *Non*, *madame*,' Madeau smiled, 'you enjoy your quiet evening without Monsieur Charles. Tomorrow there will be work for all of us.'

But Kate was regretful that she had nothing to occupy her hands and her thoughts that evening, for the time dragged slowly enough. It took her only a few minutes to slice some tomatoes, peppers and spring onions for a salad and then to beat up two eggs and pour them into sizzling butter for an omelette. She put the plates on a tray with a pot of coffee and went out to sit at one of the small tables at the side of the pool, where she ate with neither interest nor enjoyment.

It was difficult to avoid knowing that the time had come for action. It was clearly impossible for her to wait here any longer in the belief that Antoine would come and rescue her. She wasn't even sure that there was any point in his coming. It was all too late for that. And if there was to be a meeting with Antoine it must be somewhere far away from here. Yes, her mind was made up. As soon as the party was over, she would go back to London and wait. Charles had told her that a marriage such as theirs would be annulled very quickly. She would go to London, throw herself into her work and try to forget that she had ever met any of the Savoney-Morlet family.

Relieved that she had at last made up her own mind on something, she took the tray into the kitchen, washed up the few dishes and left the kitchen tidy. Restlessness made her wander about the grounds, savouring the sweet scents drifting up from Georges's small patch of herbs, mingling with all those other smells which she was beginning to identify so closely with France. With home. It gave her a stab of real pain to think how fragile her claim was to use that word here. Home must be a flat in England she had shared with Hilary, not this beautiful French country house she had shared for a brief moment with a man who was and was not her husband.

She sighed and walked back through the courtyard, glancing up to the window of Madeau's flat where the yellow light seemed so welcoming. She could imagine inside how contented they must be, planning for the arrival of the baby they had given up hope of having. Her ears caught the sound of a car accelerating up the hill and she drew back into the shadows, her heart hammering, hardly daring to hope. Then the sound reached the end of the lane—and passed, dying away in the distance.

How can you be so idiotic? Kate asked herself. But there was no answer. So firmly, determined to concentrate on her plan for the future, she went in through the front door, closing it firmly behind her.

But those long hours spent in bed in the late afternoon seemed to have robbed her for ever of the inclination to sleep. Even a swim in the pool, not a mere dalliance but an obsessive powerful crawl from one end of the pool to the other, back and forth, back and forth till her arms were exhausted, her lungs bursting in her chest with the effort, had little effect in tiring her.

She lay in the darkness of her bedroom, tossing and turning, searching for elusive sleep until with a groan of despair she sat up and switched on the bedside lamp. If she couldn't sleep then perhaps she might read. Throwing back the covers on her bed, she went to the door, then without waiting to put on either slippers or a wrap she ran swiftly downstairs to where she had seen some copies of the latest American fashion magazines. She remembered that in one of them an article which had interested her had caught her eye.

But as soon as she pushed open the door of the sitting-room she hesitated. Light was spilling from somewhere. Not from any of the lamps in the room but faintly, from some higher source. Of course—she felt a throb of pain—Charles must be back. After listening for every sound she had decided that he had not yet returned, but she had been wrong. Was she ever anything else?

Carefully she slipped into the room and moving silently reached the small table where she was able to locate the magazines she wanted. Her eyes she kept carefully averted from the upper storey, knowing that even a glimpse of him would be certain to bring a resurgence of all those feelings she was trying so hard to subdue. But her longing defeated her, for as she was about to pull the door behind her, her eyes were drawn upwards, to that gap in the sliding wall where the light escaped. She could see nothing. Nothing but the outline of his profile thrown against the pale wall. The head was leaning back, as if supported by a chair, and even as she watched, she saw a shadowy cigar raised, and placed between the parted lips. Without remembering to close the door Kate ran up to her bedroom and lay shivering between the sheets.

The next day was a blur of busyness which afterwards she could hardly remember in detail. The awkward moment of breakfast passed easily, unobtrusively, for when she went into the dining-room Madeau and Charles were involved in checking the arrangements, seeming to have time for little more than a brief glance in her direction. She was grateful, yet piqued that Charles hadn't taken time to notice her appearance in the crisp businesslike pink linen skirt and matching blouse checked in white.

'You slept well?' When Madeau left the room he turned to her with a dark searching look.

'Yes.' Perhaps it was the ease with which the lie came

to her lips that brought the faint colour to her cheeks, but she tried to regard him calmly as she raised her steaming cup in both hands. 'And you?'

'I always sleep well.'

Kate didn't ask him if that meant smoking at one-thirty in the morning, and he immediately went on to speak about what he meant to do that day.

'We'll have drinks on the terrace first. Then the meal will be laid out in here, Kate.' He waved an arm round the large dining room. 'I'll leave that side to you and Madeau. She's pretty efficient and will tell you anything you want to know.' Kate's stab of annoyance that he would assume that she needed guidance was almost immediately dispersed. 'I'd like you to do the flowers. Yours always look special.' He paused, his eyes wandering over her face and seeming, she thought with a hint of panic, to come to rest rather more frequently than she wished on her mouth. 'And perhaps this is an evening for something just a bit out of the ordinary.' She wasn't certain whether or not she saw a glint of sardonic amusement in his face, he turned away so abruptly. 'Oh, and by the way,' he paused at the door, frowning over a piece of paper he held in his hand, 'I'm glad your hair is back to normal.' The door closed behind him and she could hear him call to Madeau as he walked across the hall.

She was trembling as she pushed her chair away from the table and ran across to the mirror above the sideboard. Her hand actually shook as she touched the gold-brown silky skeins as they tumbled about her shoulders, she spoke a few words of gratitude that she had spent so much time after her swim last night shampooing, conditioning and then blow-drying her hair. Not, she assured herself as she looked at her parted lips, her tender expression, that she had meant to excite Charles's interest. All she wanted to do was wipe that superior smile off Françoise's face when she came to the party tonight, to make a great impression before, like an impressionist's stooge in a stage show, she disappeared in a flash of light.

For the rest of the day she had little time to admire herself in the mirror or to ponder on the effect she would have on Charles's friends who would come expecting to meet the girl Françoise had described. There was little time for anything in the excitement and stress of preparing for the guests who would be arriving that evening. When she had helped Madeau and her sister Antoinette—whose name didn't cause Kate so much as a pang—in the kitchen, when she had advised Georges who was precariously balanced on a ladder draping coloured lights round the pool, she went out into the garden and began to pick huge bunches of flowers with which she intended decorating the hall and main rooms of the house, putting them for an hour or two in the coolness of one of the outbuildings where they rested up to their necks in baths of water.

But the hours seemed simply to fly past, and at the last minute there was a panic when it seemed that the guests would be arriving while there were still a hundred jobs to be completed. At last everything was ready and they even had time to congregate in the kitchen for cups of tea and some sandwiches which Antoinette had been busy preparing for the last half hour.

'I'm hungry.' Kate leaned back, supporting herself against the table. 'And these are delicious, Antoinette.' She listened while Madeau translated what she had said, trying to pretend that no compulsion was pulling her eyes to the tall figure who lounged against the wall opposite, drinking his tea.

'I think we were all hungry.' He levered himself from the wall and placed his cup on the draining board. 'It seems a long time since the soup and cheese we had at lunch time. And I've worked harder than I've done for a long time.'

Kate got up and taking her cup to the sink washed and dried both of them. She turned towards the door when with what she considered sheer effrontery, Charles caught her lightly round the waist, swinging her about so that she would have lost her balance had she not put her hands to his shoulders. 'You can eat as much as you like tonight, *chérie*.' He smiled down into her startled eyes. 'Although perhaps the guests will be surprised if the bride throws herself on the food as if she is starving!'

There was a sound of laughter from the others as Madeau translated again, then into the silence, for the benefit of the three who were watching the scene Kate spoke sweetly. 'But then I'm not exactly a bride, *chéri*. Am I?' She smiled up into his face, then detaching herself firmly, 'I must go or I'll be late.'

She knew that he held the door for her and followed her through into the hall. She knew that his eyes were on her as she paused by the huge arrangement of delphiniums, strikingly beautiful in the old copper jug; that he watched her as she moved to the staircase and began to climb.

'Kate.' Something in his voice made her falter, then turn without meaning to do either. She said nothing, but stood looking down at him, the deep violet of her eyes tortured as she tried to thrust aside feelings that she knew were futile. She waited, the moments seeming to stretch between them until he spoke again, and then it was with a dismissive shrug, a faint smile. 'Oh, nothing.'

'You were going to say,' for once she felt that the initiative was with her, 'something about what I should wear.' Now hers were the lips that were mocking and she felt his eyes on them. 'Weren't you?

'How clever you are, Kate.' He came forward to the rail and leaned against it, looking up at her admiringly. 'Just like any long-married wife, knowing her husband's desires so well.' He smiled at the faint colour in her cheeks. 'Perhaps I was going to say something of the like. Now that I know you understand my wishes so well, perhaps there's no need.'

Drawn by a force outside herself, Kate leaned down, putting the back of one hand against his cheek. 'Then can I ask you, Charles,' her voice was soft and tender, 'to do something in return for me? Please shave. Because if there's one thing I can't stand,' her voice grew just a little sharp at the same moment as she drew her hand away, hearing the faint rasp of his beard, 'is dancing with a man who has a cheek like a bed of nails!' And without looking down at him again she ran quickly to the top of the stairs, ignoring the faint deep sound of laughter that followed her.

But when they met again neither was in any mood for feeble witticisms, each was too conscious, too vibrantly aware of the other's presence to risk the shattering of the tautly controlled emotion that held them.

As she walked slowly downstairs, Kate knew that she

was about to give the performance of her life, the show that she would remember till the end. And for that leading rôle she was dressed like a star.

The dress that Kulu had made for a rich American might have been designed for Kate instead of coming to her because of a whim of the original customer. There was a wide circular yoke encrusted with glittering beads, long ruby-coloured bugles, gold sequins, flat discs of jet and from the yoke hung a cascade of pleats reaching to her ankles. The pale pink drew attention to the honey bloom of her skin and the diaphanous softness of the sheer cotton floated about her as she moved.

Never before had Kate taken such trouble with her appearance. The shining hair was pulled softly back from her face and piled with deceptive casualness just above her nape but with one or two wisps being allowed to escape and curl softly about her face. Her eyelids were cleverly shadowed with a soft grey colour and her lips had been touched with palest pink.

About her wrist she had clasped a gilt glittery bracelet which drew attention from her face, then to her slender feet, encased in impossibly high gold sandals. She held her breath as she reached the bottom step, and the figure she knew had been watching her descent came forward to meet her.

They stared at each other, then Kate found her hand taken, Charles's lips pressed against it briefly before it was held to his smooth freshly shaven cheek. 'I hope, my beautiful Kate, that I please you half as well as you please me.' When he had spoken the silence throbbed between them. Without taking her eyes from his face she could not mistake the tall litheness of his figure, nor ignore the sophisticated perfection of the smooth dark dinner jacket, the frill of the shirt front edged with black.

'Come with me, Kate. I have something for you.' And she found herself being led, with an urgency that seemed to have little to do with the imminent arrival of guests to the small study which opened from a short corridor off the hall and which Kate had seen only once.

Inside the room she stood, watching while he went over to the small antique desk beside the window, opened the drawer and took out a small box, returning to her and holding it towards her.

'What is it?' She felt that she daren't take it, that she had no right to become further involved with this man, that whatever was inside that box would only make it more difficult for her to stick to her resolve.

'Open it, Kate.' His voice was deep and warm and insinuating so that without further consideration she pressed the button that held the blue leather lid in position.

The ring she looked down at was blazing with the glory of a perfect sapphire—so perfect that even as she knew that she must not take it she found admiration impossible to resist. 'It's beautiful!' she exclaimed.

'Then let me put it on for you.' He reached for the box, imprisoning her hand at the same time.

'No.' She tightened her fingers, looking at him with frightened appealing eyes.

'You must, Kate.' He seemed to share the tension that invaded her at his touch. 'It's natural that my wife would have an engagement ring. I insist.' Gently he opened her now unresisting fingers and she watched him slip the ring on the finger where the plain gold band had been placed a week before. Then she trembled as he took her fingers to his mouth and kissed them. 'A perfect match for your eyes, Kate.' But as he spoke he seemed to have no interest in the costly jewel.

CHAPTER NINE

THEN before there was time to even think of anything else they heard the arrival of the first guests.

Kate's first impression was that all Charles's friends were rich cosmopolitans who jet-setted round the world and who spoke transatlantic English almost as well as Charles himself did. She was introduced to men accompanied by beautiful elegant wives whose conversation was interspersed with references to Lagos and Riyadh, Algiers and Tehran, New York and Hong Kong.

'But tell us about yourself, Kate.' A short dark man whose name she thought was Claude admired her over the rim of his champagne glass, tried to draw her out. 'It was such a surprise to hear that Charles had found a wife. And you are a very pleasant surprise indeed. I imagined someone quite different. Why is that, do you think, Lise?' He turned briefly to his wife, a tiny fair-haired girl.

Lise shrugged and smiled at Kate. 'I can't say. I suppose I just got the wrong impression from what Françoise said.' Kate caught an exchange of looks between the women and was grateful when Charles came up behind them, slipping his hand into Kate's and smiling down at her.

'I'm asking Kate why you've been hiding her for so long.' Claude spoke to his host although his eyes were still on Kate's face. 'It wasn't fair on the rest of us.'

'That was what I liked about the idea,' Charles replied smoothly.

'But where did you meet?' One of the other women seemed intrigued. 'Was it in France? Or London?'

'It's all a bit complicated, Nini, but in fact we met in France. Perhaps some day we'll feel like telling you the whole story, but at the moment we feel inclined to keep it to ourselves.'

'Sounds very romantic!'

'It was.' Kate thought it was time she took some part in the conversation, and anyway it gave her the opportunity to look lovingly up into Charles's face. 'It was the most romantic, unexpected meeting you can imagine.' She faltered a little as she saw the expression in his eyes and was glad that a flurry of new arrivals gave them the opportunity to leave the group round the pool and go forward to meet some older people who had just come and were being shown through the french doors by Antoinette.

Gravely, courteously Charles introduced her to them, explaining carefully who each was; Monsieur and Madame Perrette farmed the land adjoining, Monsieur de Warens was the local vet and Madame Gardillou lived in the large house at the far end of the village. As none of these people spoke any English Kate had to content herself with a very limited conversation, using the words she was gradually picking up from Madeau and because of that trying particularly to make them feel welcome. She suspected that they, in their slightly old-fashioned formal clothes, might feel a little awkward with the younger, more trendy guests, and that was another reason for showing extra warmth. She sensed that Charles had the same idea and was grateful when he took the trouble to do some translating. She listened to a lengthy discussion, suspected from the way all eyes were concentrated on her that she was the subject, and turned enquiringly to Charles when it ended.

'I am being congratulated, Kate, on my choice of a bride. They can quite understand why I chose an English girl.'

'Oh . . .' Kate fluttered her eyelashes and blushed. '*Merci, mesdames et messieurs. Et moi aussi.*' She struggled to find the words. '*Je suis très contente avec mon français.*'

'Bravo!' Monsieur de Warens clapped his hands and reaching for his glass raised it to them both. '*A votre santé, madame. Et Charles.*'

Soon though there was little time to do more than welcome the guests as they arrived so quickly, one group after another until the terrace by the pool was crowded and the air was loud with the sound of conversation and laughter. Almost the last person to arrive was Françoise, with just a step behind her a short dapper man of middle age.

Kate was standing by the open french door when they came through the sitting room and she stepped forward with a welcoming smile, her hand held out, knowing that Charles was a mere step behind her. As her eyes and Françoise's met, Kate knew that for a moment she had not been recognised. There was total absence of response in the pale eyes which almost at once flicked away from the girl towards the tall figure just behind her.

'Charles!' The shrill voice was affectionate and she stood on tiptoe to brush his cheek with her lips. Then she noticed Charles had his hand on Kate's elbow and her eyes moved to her face, still with that blank expression of incomprehension. Another quick glance to Charles and back again before understanding dawned, a look of anger instantly disguised in a smile. 'And Kate. How wonderful you look tonight, *chérie*!' Colour rose in the visitor's face as she wondered if she had betrayed too much of her feelings.

'And you too, Françoise.' At least in that Kate thought she could be truthful. 'That's a simply sensational gown.'

Françoise looked down at the gold lamé cheongsam, skin-tight and with the skirt slit to the knee on one side. 'Thank you. It's one I had made in Hong Kong a few months ago.' She seemed to remember she had brought someone with her and looked round to where Charles and her partner were having a casual conversation. 'Emil, this is the new Madame Savoney-Morlet.' There was a trace of sarcastic waspishness in her voice that made Kate wince, but she smiled as she held out her hand to the short stout man who was looking at her.

'*Enchanté, madame.*' He held her hand, bowing over it. 'You are not the lady I expected.' He spoke with such a strong accent that Kate had difficulty understsnding his words. 'The picture you drew, *chérie*,' he smiled at Françoise, 'made me think of someone quite different.'

Françoise shrugged without replying, her eyes searching the faces of the guests for someone she knew, and at the same moment Kate's eyes met Charles's, surprising there a tiny glint of amusement—as if he too were remembering the day when she had poured so much oil on her hair and had dressed in her oldest jeans and blouse. The shared recollection gave her a warm comfortable glow.

The party seemed to be a considerable success, if noise and laughter were any guide. Kate circulated constantly, never feeling completely at ease except when Charles was by her side, but when his hand was on her arm, when they were presenting the picture of perfect romantic bliss, all her nervousness disappeared. He seemed to sense this, for he was rarely far from her side, always finding the role of devoted husband one which sat on his shoulders with ease.

The food was predictably perfect, the *boeuf en gêlée* cut into thin pink slices which simply melted in the mouth and the array of delicious salads offering a bewildering choice. Kate was so busy seeing that the guests had all that they wanted that she forgot that she was hungry till Charles appeared by her side holding out a plate with a careful selection of salads and meat.

'Come.' The dark eyes entertained no refusal. 'You must be exhausted. I've found a nice quiet spot where we can eat in peace.'

'But won't they . . . Won't your guests expect you to be with them?'

'I think they're all happy now. They're meeting lots of friends, they're all eating and drinking merrily enough. And that reminds me, I notice that you haven't had a glass of champagne. Come on, Kate.' And holding his own plate in one hand, leading Kate with the other, he took her to a small window seat in one of the corridors at the back of the hall.

It was clear enough that he had made some previous arrangements, for on the sill were two tall glasses and an ice bucket with a bottle of champagne. Kate sat quietly, waiting while he eased the cork from the bottle and poured the sparkling liquid into the waiting glasses.

'To you, Kate.' He stood looking down at her, his face hidden from her in the shadowy darkness, only the white of his shirt front gleaming but faintly coloured from the lights that hung about the pool outside the window.

'To you, Charles.' Her voice was low with an aching sadness and she felt like weeping while knowing that she must not. She sipped the wine, glad when he sat down on the seat beside her and began to shake out the large linen napkin.

'That's better.' If she was moved by the occasion he seemed remarkably calm as he emptied his glass and reached again for the bottle. Kate followed his lead, feeling much more cheerful as the refreshing wine raced through her veins, holding out her glass again for replenishing.

During the meal they spoke little, but there was a companionable quality about their silence, as if they were just any other couple relaxing during a successful party. When Kate had finished her main course, Charles removed the plates, returning a few minutes later with two large goblets of sugared strawberries and a plate with a selection of cheeses.

'Tonight I shall do it the English way and have the fruit first. Then we can share the cheese.'

And that was what they did, Charles handing her cubes of cheese speared on a fork which he selected as if he were choosing the nicest pieces specially for her, just as any good husband should. Kate was glad that the passion she felt for him had quietened, that he did nothing to fan it into that burning, frustrating, destructive emotion which had engulfed them the previous day. For the moment she was content with the bitter-sweetness of just sitting beside Charles, quietly enjoying his company, exchanging unimportant little remarks. And the realisation that the pleasure of this evening must last a very long time brought a feeling of nostalgia as if she had already gone.

When they had finished, Charles held out a hand to help her to her feet, looking at her with an expression that made her wonder, just for a brief moment, if he too was savouring this time that he knew must be fleeting. But then he smiled, wryly, holding her for a breathless moment by her fingertips.

'Time to get back to duty.'

And they had rejoined their guests, mingling with them as they drank coffee and finally all gravitating in the direction of the sitting room where the carpet had been removed so that it was possible to dance on the smooth floor of the ancient barn. In the corner beside the open windows the large stereo was playing soft music, mostly the sweet old-fashioned kind but interspersed with a few reggae tapes.

'Shall we?' Charles's arm was already round her waist but he turned her towards him smiling into her eyes. 'If we don't none of the others will, that's certain.'

Kate drew in a sharp breath and saw the expression on his face change, the smile fade while something, a warning flashed in the darkness of his eyes. But before they could move out on to the cleared portion at the edge of the room, someone banged a metal tray and there was a sudden lull in the animated conversation.

Monsieur de Warens was standing in the centre of the room, obviously determined to make a speech of congratulation. Kate stood, her eyes moving round the faces of the guests, seeing them laugh, finding that she was blushing even though she understood little of what was being said. Lounging back in a chair, Emil sitting on the side, his arm extending along the back of the seat, sat Françoise, her lips unsmiling, her eyes fixed with a very hungry look on Charles's face. Then, as she became conscious of Kate's scrutiny, the pale eyes moved over, staring with such an expression of jealous hatred that Kate shivered suddenly.

'Be calm, *chérie*.' She heard the whisper in her ear and looked up gratefully just as the speech of congratulation came to an end.

'Thank you,' she whispered up at him, and looked round as Georges came from behind them with two glasses on a silver tray. Without thinking about it she took the glass, listened to the brief reply Charles made, and turned to raise her glass to him in response to his salute.

'To you, Kate.' His whisper made her eyes fill with tears, and to her dismay he took a handkerchief from his pocket and wiped her eyes carefully. Round about them the noise of laughter and clapping drowned any words that they might have to say to each other and miraculously the volume of the music was turned up so that the tantalising notes of a dreamy waltz filled the room. She sipped the wine and then allowed Charles to take the glass from her hand and give it with his own to Georges who was hovering nearby.

As his arm held her to him, her eyes were raised to his, uncaring that he might be able to decipher her expression while their feet moved in time to the music, quite as if they had danced together a hundred times before. If others joined them on the floor neither Kate nor Charles seemed to notice. There was such ecstasy in the smooth movement of their bodies, such pleasure in the touch of his cheek against hers. The scent of his cologne rose in her nostrils, exciting her as it always did, and she lowered her eyes, her head drooping towards his shoulder. When the music changed to something more vibrant and exciting, stars gleamed in her eyes as they faced each other, gyrating to the intense pulsating throb, twisting like supple jungle cats, turning but always coming back to face each other, eyes searching.

It was too sensuous and provocative to be endured, so perhaps it was as well that they were interrupted, that Claude cut in on them saying something about claiming a dance with the bride and at the same time Charles turned away in response to the insistent hand that Lise put on his sleeve. After that Kate seemed to be claimed for every dance and she saw that Charles was dutifully dancing with the older women guests, appearing to think that the younger women were being well enough looked after by his guests.

Until he danced with Françoise, that was! And although she tried hard not to notice, Kate could hardly avoid seeing that he spent much more time with her than with any of the others. She saw his head lowered as he listened to what she was saying, her animated face turned upwards, appealingly, it seemed to Kate. Once she happened to see the man who had arrived with Françoise and he was watching them with an intense expression as they circled round the floor.

Kate, who had just relinquished one partner pleading exhaustion, stopped to speak to him. 'You don't care for dancing?'

'I care for it.' He shrugged and smiled, transforming his rather dull face with a flash of humour. 'But alas, I have no sense of rhythm—or so Françoise tells me.' His tense expression sought out her figure on the floor again. 'The thing is, Madame Savoney-Morlet, that when I was a young man I had no time to learn dancing. I was poor and had to make my way in the world. Now, I think it is too late to begin.'

'Of course it isn't.' Kate felt a sudden surge of sympathy for the man, who seemed as out of place in this gathering as she felt. 'Would you like to try this one?' She held her head to one side, beating out the rhythm with one finger. 'It really doesn't matter what you do to this music. You can just move from one foot to the other. Nobody notices.'

'Very well.' He grinned at her with a faintly conspiratorial expression. 'If you would be so good, *madame.*'

But just as they were walking on to the floor Françoise, apparently deserted by Charles and not happy about it, appeared in front of them, blocking their way. Her eyes travelled slowly over Kate's face before moving on to Emil. 'I think we had better go, Emil. It is late and I feel tired. Thank you for a lovely party, *madame.*'

'I'm glad you could come.' Kate's manner gave no indication of the annoyance she felt at the other woman's barely veiled rudeness.

'It was so kind of you to come.'

'Then *au 'voir, madame.*' Emil bowed over her hand. 'Our dance, I'm afraid, must wait for another time. Perhaps for your sake it was just as well!'

After that there was a general thinning out of the crowd, and the last to say goodnight were the ones who had arrived first, Claude and Lise. He held Kate's hand for just a fraction longer than necessary and she thought that there was a particular message in his eyes when he looked at her.

'I suggested a midnight swim, Kate, but your husband thought it wasn't such a good idea.'

'Besides which,' Charles's voice was deep and had a faint warning note, 'midnight has long since gone. It is after two o'clock.'

'*Oui*. Come now, Claude.' Lise pulled impatiently at his arm. 'I am tired.' She yawned, showing her pretty even teeth.

'Very well, *chérie*.' He sighed indulgently. '*Bon soir*, Kate. *Bon soir*, Charles.' And a few minutes later they had driven out of the courtyard, leaving it empty.

Kate walked into the kitchen, surprised to see that it looked very much as usual, all the dishes and most of the glasses having been washed and replaced in their cupboards, all the surfaces wiped clean. Georges turned from the sink where he was rinsing a few last things under a tap and smiled at her.

'Oh, Georges, thank you.' Then as Charles followed her into the room she turned to him. 'Would you tell Georges how grateful I am? And I was going to suggest that you tell them they needn't come in tomorrow. They deserve a break after all the work they've done and I can tidy the house and make some food if we feel hungry.'

'Sure?' The dark eyes questioned her enigmatically. Then as she confirmed with a brief little nod she heard him explain to Georges, heard the man's obvious pleasure at the suggestion. With a murmured goodnight to Georges Kate slipped out of the kitchen, pausing for a moment in the hall before, almost by instinct, she followed the sound of music that was still coming from the sitting-room.

She was standing by the window when she heard the door open and footsteps cross the wooden floor. 'How do you put this off?' She moved towards the stereo, glad to do something that would keep her mind occupied.

'Leave it for a moment. Come and sit down. You must be tired, Kate.'

Reluctantly, willingly, she couldn't decide which, Kate turned round and walked into the centre of the room, avoiding his eyes until something impelled her to turn and look at him. There was a curious expression on his face, unsmiling yet soft, gentle as he took her hand to lead her to a seat.

But instead of sitting, he held her hand close to his chest, his other arm circled her waist and their feet began to move in time to the music. Kate gazed up at him, thinking of nothing but how she loved him, forgetting that yesterday he had rejected her with withering scorn, forgetting her newly reached determination to sever her links with him as soon as possible.

Then they were no longer dancing, they were standing together, his hands were linked about her waist, hers had crept up to loop themselves about his neck. Kate had one thought in her mind, one urge in her body, and because all words like caution and discretion and even self-protection had simply faded from her mind she obeyed her instinct.

At first there was no response as her lips trembled beneath his. She closed her eyes, leaning against him, murmuring his name, stroking the back of his neck with one finger. And then the fire that had smouldered between them for so long burst into consuming flames as his mouth bruised hers with a fierce, possessive hardness, his fingers moved over her body, moulding her pliant form to his.

'Kate! My Kate.' Even her name was a caress as he spoke it, sweet torment to her body, and a faint moan escaped from her lips as she surrendered to him body and soul.

'Kate?' He held her from him for a moment, cupping her face in his hands, searching her face with a dark intensity which made her tremble. There was no doubt in her mind that he was asking a question, seeking a response in her eyes, eyes that were heavy with longing in the soft lighting. Her lips parted softly, invitingly, and she rejoiced in the faint triumphant laugh that sounded in her ears in that moment before he swept her from her feet, carrying her exultantly from the room.

CHAPTER TEN

KATE lay in the moonwashed bedroom listening to Charles's even, contented breathing by her side. She smiled to herself, an expression of sheer joy and contentment as carefully she turned round so that she was lying watching his face. It was relaxed in sleep, the dark hair falling across his forehead, so infinitely dear to her that she raised herself on one elbow and gently kissed the closed eyelids.

'Kate.' He murmured her name, the eyes opened for a second to look lazily at her, smiling sleepily. 'Kate.' His hand reached out, resting for an instant against her cheek, drifting down her throat to her breast, and then sleep overpowered him again.

She lay watching the rise and fall of the darkly tanned chest, longing to reach out a hand to touch the springy hair, only restrained by an unwillingness to disturb him again. Tears of pleasure stung her eyes as she remembered the unbelievable joy that the night had brought her. And to him.

There had been no hesitation about their coming together after that questioning embrace in the sitting-room when the guests had left them. The fire that had consumed her had found a match in his, but, as if aware of her inexperience, he had shown restraint and infinite gentleness that first time.

After that he had made love to her with fierce abandon, so that time and again together they reached a
giddy height of ecstasy Kate could never have imagined.
And together they descended, floating down from the
enchanted planes where their mingling flesh had taken
them to this plateau of sweet fulfilment.

Kate sighed and closed her eyes, allowing sleep to
wash over her. And she dreamed, now without terror,
and the man who strode through her unconscious
thoughts was no longer a stranger, but the man who was
in truth her husband.

The room was bright with sunshine when she stirred.
First she gave a contented little sigh and turned over
on the pillow, reaching out her hand across the empty
bed. It was a moment before her eyes shot open, deeply
violet and troubled when she realised that she was alone
there. For a time she was too shocked to move, her
heart hammered against her ribs as the awful impression crossed her mind.

Surely, surely it hadn't all been a dream? She
couldn't have imagined . . . She pushed herself to a sitting position, then realising that she was naked, she
slipped down with a smile, yet feeling the warmth in
her cheeks. At the same instant she saw, lying on the
floor by the side of the bed, the discarded dress that she
had tossed aside with such unseemly haste.

Her blush deepened and her eyes moved across to the
door, her heart bounding when she saw, folded over a
chair, Charles's dark dinner jacket, the white shirt a
crumpled heap beside it. So it hadn't been a dream; her
heart quietened and for a time she was content to lie
there, her lips curved in a smile of recollection.

But then she remembered that she and Charles were to restore the house to its normal condition. Besides, she couldn't bear life an instant longer without seeing him. Quickly she rose, decided that she would have a quick swim in the pool before she made Charles some breakfast. Then they would begin to repair the ravages of the sitting-room. She smiled again, willing at last to admit to herself that after last night the prospect of appearing before him in another new swimsuit was . . . intriguing.

The impact of the suit was, Kate decided as she viewed the result in the mirror, worth every penny she had paid for it. It was stunningly simple, stunningly daring, the halter neckline plunging revealingly to the jewelled buckle of the low-slung belt. Its colour, brilliant dramatic violet that matched her eyes, had been the first thing that attracted her, and she felt excited as she snatched up a broad-brimmed black straw hat, pushed her sunglasses on to her nose and ran downstairs.

Barefoot she walked through the sitting room on to the terrace, pausing by the open door, her eyes searching for some sight of the only person she wanted to see just then. The heat hung heavy over the sheltered corner and Kate walked slowly over the hot paving stones, stood looking down into the clear blue water for a moment, then stooping, splashed the surface with one languid hand.

The water shimmered and when it stilled she saw a reflection behind her own and straightened, turning slowly, shyly towards him. He was wearing pale trousers, a cream silk shirt open to the waist, sleeves rolled back to show the strong forearms. As her eyes swept over him she noticed that his hair was crisp and damp, and irrationally was aware of a stab of disappointment.

'Kate.' He regarded her warily for a moment before stepping forward, his eyes sweeping over her blushing cheeks, lingering on the cloud of golden-brown hair that fell to her shoulders. The firm lips curved into a smile of greeting. 'Kate,' he said again.

'I hoped you might feel like having a swim,' she faltered, 'but you look as if you . . .'

'No, I had a shower, Kate. I . . . left you about half an hour ago.' As he watched her increasing colour his smile grew wider and one hand came out to pluck the sunglasses from her face. 'I told you, Kate my sweet, that I always want to be able to see your eyes. And as to swimming with you, I feel the opportunity is one that I can hardly resist.' He came close, looking down at her with a gentle expression while his hand circled her neck. 'As I find almost everything about you hard to resist this morning, my Kate.' He paused and grew more thoughtful. 'Impossible even. I'll be down in two minutes if you'll wait . . .' He grinned then, turned away and strode into the house.

Kate, surrounded by a miasma of love and joy and a dozen emotions which she would have thought were impossible to experience at that time in the morning, sank on to one of the chairs, her fingers reaching for a swimming cap she had left there a day or two earlier. But she had little time to think, for Charles was back as soon as he had promised and he casually tossed her one of the towels he was carrying.

'Here, *chérie*.' The old sardonic smile touched his mouth. 'I see you forgot to bring one down. I would like to think it was because you were too dazzled by love

to be aware of what you were doing, but . . .' his eyes
had narrowed a little, he was watching her with an
intensity which she found puzzling, then she understood that he was waiting to hear her answer the implicit
question.

'I should have thought . . .' Her voice quivered a
little and under his searching eyes she grew shy again.
'Charles . . .'

'*Oui, chérie*?' His tone was gently prompting.

'I . . .'

But before she could say any more they heard the
sharp tapping sound of heels coming round the corner
of the house, the subdued murmur of voices, and Kate
paused while they both looked up, regretting the
interruption.

And into view, looking as immaculate as she always
did, dressed in pale green linen, every strand of her
blonde curls lacquered into a halo, stepped Françoise.
She stopped when she saw them standing so closely, so
intimately together, and a strange self-satisfied smile
crossed her face. Kate only glimpsed it before the visitor
turned to the man who had followed her, automatically
she took in the tall dark figure. Then she realised that
his eyes were devouring her, that he was stepping
towards her. The name that was on his lips was her own.

The picture unfolded in slow motion before her eyes.
She heard her own gasp of disbelief, felt her legs begin
to fold beneath her as Antoine crossed the few remain-
ing yards, hands outstretched. But it was as if he were
running and running and never coming any closer.
Behind him Françoise smiled, tenderly to Charles,
triumphantly towards Kate.

Before Antoine could reach her Charles touched her arm, a chair was hooked close to her so that she could sit. Despairingly she looked up into the handsome, charming features, unresisting she allowed him to take her hands to his lips, heard a sob but couldn't understand whether it was her own or his.

'Kate!' There was a sparkle of tears in his eyes, his voice shook with emotion as he spoke her name. 'Kate, my darling!'

'Wasn't this a surprise!' Françoise's voice, less soothing even than usual, cut through Kate's thoughts. 'Last night I ran Emil back to his hotel. Then when I was driving back home I saw someone fiddling with a broken-down car by the roadside. Of course I recognised him at once and stopped. I . . .'

'Be quiet, Françoise!' Charles's voice encouraged no defiance. Grimly he faced his cousin. 'What do you want, Antoine?'

The blank look of incomprehension on Antoine's features might have been amusing in other circumstances, but no one showed any inclination to smile. Even Françoise appeared to have lost any such tendency, although she was clearly missing nothing.

'What do I want?' Antoine gave a slight laugh. 'What do you think I want, Charles? I want Kate. I want my wife.' And as he spoke, he leaned forward to pull her to her feet. Kate stared into his eyes, vaguely wondering how she had thought that he and Charles were so much alike. They were both dark, of course, but this was a weak, boyish face and she doubted that he would ever develop the strength and power of his elder cousin. Beside Charles he looked slight and immature. Kate tried to blot out from her mind what was happening, and suddenly the earth began a crazy, swaying motion which made her feel giddy.

It was Charles's voice that she heard cry a warning whose words she could not understand. In that last moment before she lost any awareness of what was happening she sensed that Antoine was thrust aside, that it was Charles's strong arms that swept her off the ground. Just as they had last . . .

Kate had no idea how long she had been unconscious, but when she came to she was lying on her own bed, in her own room, and someone was pressing a cold damp cloth to her forehead. She opened her eyes, felt the room sway for a moment, then steady. Françoise's voice spoke, soothingly, insincerely.

'How are you, Kate?' A film of green floated, then materialised into the girl Kate disliked so much.

'All right now.' Strangely the lie did not stick in her throat, but she turned her head abruptly, trying to hide the tears that stung so painfully.

'Good.' There was a note of satisfaction in Françoise's voice that made Kate grapple for control, then turn defiantly to face her.

'I'm afraid, Kate, you've allowed yourself to be used by Antoine and Charles. If only you had known, my dear!' She sat down on the edge of the bed, her eyes moving away from the girl on the bed, searching the room, while Kate burned at the remembrance of Charles's clothes lying so casually on the chair.

'I don't think I've been used.' Kate forced herself to sit up in bed, feeling ridiculously at a disadvantage in her swimming suit. 'Do you mind?' She pointed to the wrap lying on the floor where it had fallen, at the same time feeling relieved that she had taken time to hang away the dress, the beautiful pink dress she had worn last night. 'Thank you.' She pulled the light robe about her shoulders.

'Oh, these Savoney-Morlets, you do not know them, *ma chère*.' Without asking for permission Françoise pulled a packet of cigarettes from her handbag and lit up. 'Charming, I agree.' She pulled the smoke deep into her lungs. 'Too charming, perhaps. But they would use any means to get their own way.' She smiled insincerely at the girl on the bed.

'I have known Charles a long time, Kate. I have seen how he tried to control the bitterness . . . You do not know. My family befriended him when first he came. My father helped him, regarded him as a son in some ways. But all the time I was aware that deep inside he had never forgiven or forgotten. In these old families, the idea of inheritance is very deep. You know,' she studied the glowing end of her cigarette with great interest, 'you know, I believe Charles would do anything to get back at his aunt—the person whom he blames above all for the loss of what he thinks should be his.'

Without speaking Kate stared at the older woman. Now she was beginning to collect her thoughts and her most pressing problem was to find out just what Françoise knew about the present situation. Had Antoine explained exactly what had happened? Or had he been discreet, revealing only what he felt suited him at that moment? She tried to remember exactly what Antoine had said when first he had come forward to meet her.

'Kate, my darling!' She remembered that. And then she struggled with the fog that seemed to have invaded her brain and it cleared when she heard Charles asking Antoine why he had come. 'I want Kate. I want my wife.' The words echoed in her head so that she knew for certain she was not imagining it. So . . . possibly . . . Françoise believed that she and Antoine were married. It was all becoming so confusing.

'You know what I mean, don't you, Kate?'

'What?' She looked up into Françoise's speculative face, trying to remember what she had been saying. 'I'm sorry . . .' She didn't entirely trust the friendly expression on the other girl's face.

'I was saying . . .' Françoise hesitated and a faint colour stained her cheeks, '. . . that Charles is not the man to miss the opportunity of righting what he thinks of as the wrong that he thinks was done to him.'

Kate stared, trying to understand what this conversation was leading up to, but she didn't speak.

'And you must not blame yourself, Kate. We all know just how irresistible he can be when he tries.'

'Blame myself?'

'Yes. And Antoine need never know. If Charles's scheme did work,' there was a momentary return of her old acid manner, but it was almost instantly disguised by a vague sympathetic smile, 'if by chance you are *enceinte*, then it will still be a Savoney-Morlet who inherits the estate. And,' now there was no disguising her animosity. 'I've no doubt you will have the memory of a few idyllic days here with Charles.' Her laugh made Kate shudder.

'Would you mind going downstairs?' It was with difficulty Kate controlled herself. 'Would you tell them that I'll be down in a few minutes?'

'Of course, *chérie*.' Françoise bent to pick up her

handbag. 'Take your time. I shall keep them busy till you come down. It has all been something . . .'

'Please,' the coldness of her voice shocked Kate, 'would you go.'

And without another word Françoise flounced round and went out, closing the door behind her with exaggerated consideration.

Kate slid her feet on to the floor without getting up from the bed. Her head was bowed in a gesture of despondency that only partially reflected the despair which possessed her. No matter what she had endured in the past days surely this was a blow from which she would never recover.

Dully she turned her face to look at the pillows where last night they had lain together. Even that had all been part of the plan. She could see it all now. Charles with his experience had carefully brought her to a pitch where she was putty in his hands, ready, anxious even, to jump into bed with him. And if questioned he could even say that she had encouraged him. Kate raised her clenched fists and pressed them to her closed eyelids. Was there no end to her foolishness? How could she?

She was trembling when at last she got up from the bed, but a determination to finish the episode as quickly as possible gave her the strength to pull off her swimsuit and dress in a black and white cotton voile dress which she snatched from a hanger without looking at it. She stood in front of the mirror, pulling in the wide belt about her slender waist, pushed back the tumbled hair from her face, then slipped her bare feet into high heelless cork soles.

There was a murmur of voices from the sitting room as she crossed the hall and she stood with her hand on the door knob, irrationally reluctant to go inside until she had to force herself. The sound of her feet tapping on the wood seemed to be coming from a great distance, her eyes had difficulty focusing on the group sitting round the coffee table. The two men stood up, Antoine came towards her, but it was Charles whom her eyes sought.

He was watching her, a close brooding expression on his face as if he were displeased with her. Kate felt her hands caught in Antoine's, evaded his mouth, but could not escape the pressure of his cheek on hers. At once she was taken back to London by the familiar scent of his cologne.

'Kate—darling!' The dark eyes searched her face suspiciously as he held her at arm's length. 'Come and sit down.' He led her over to a settee and sat beside her, still clinging to one of her hands.

'When did you come back from Australia?' She had to force her lips to move.

'Last night, Kate. I should have arrived in the afternoon, but the plane was delayed and it was late before we touched down in Limoges. Then the car broke down.' He sighed and smiled at her, another reminder of those Alice in Wonderland days when they had first met. 'It was meant to be such a surprise, *chérie*. And if it hadn't been for Françoise coming along the road . . .' He cast a grateful glance across the table. 'Even then I was anxious to come straight up here. But she insisted that it would be best to go and spend the night in her flat and she would bring me up tomorrow. I suppose she was right, it was a bit late and you would be in bed . . .'

'Besides, you were exhausted, Antoine,' Françoise

interrupted smoothly. 'Travelling all the way from Sydney, then a private flight from Paris . . .'

'Yes, we're all very grateful to you, Françoise.' It was the first time that Charles had spoken, his voice was flat and unemotional. 'It was kind of you to go to so much trouble. Now I imagine you're anxious to go back home and . . .'

'There's no hurry, Charles . . .' For once the sharpness included him.

'. . . And besides, there's a great deal to discuss. It will take a long time.' He rose, leaving her no choice but to follow his suggestion, which she did with a great deal of self-possession.

'Of course—I should have thought!' Françoise picked up her handbag from the chair and stood for a moment looking down at the younger couple. 'I hope I shall see you both before you leave. Goodbye, Antoine.' Her eyes narrowed perceptibly as she glanced at Kate. 'Goodbye, Kate.'

'Goodbye, Françoise. And thank you.' Antoine stood up, looking awkwardly from his cousin to the girl by his side. Kate made no reply and didn't look up as she heard Charles and the visitor go towards the door.

'Darling!' Antoine sat down again, putting his arms about her, pulling her against his chest. Kate lay quite still. Can this be the man, she thought, whom I loved quite madly just a few weeks ago? Or, she amended, I thought I loved madly. For at the time she had known very little about that insidious emotion.

Charles came back into the room, paused on the threshold when he saw the embrace, then walked forward purposefully. Hands on hips, he stood looking down at them till Antoine, with a rueful little laugh, put Kate away from him and rose to his feet.

'I can only thank you, Charles—once again.' He held out his hand and when his cousin made no move to take it he let it fall to his side. 'I seem to have spent my life thanking you for getting me out of trouble.'

Kate, aware of Charles's eyes on her, refused to look at him as, apart from that first appealing glance, she had done since coming into the room. She was aware that he turned away and went over to the side-table where she heard the clink of glasses, and a moment later she felt a glass being pressed into her hand.

'Drink that, Kate.' His voice was beguilingly tender. 'You have suffered a shock.' He tried to raise her chin with his finger, but she resisted and he moved away with a sigh. Kate sat looking down into the warm gold liquid and quite deliberately put the glass down on the table by her side.

'Well,' Antoine gulped at the cognac, then looked rather bewildered from one of them to the other, 'if you would like to get your things, Kate . . .'

'What?' She leaned back in her seat, looking up at him but still avoiding that other more penetrating face.

'I've arranged to hire another car. So we can take your things . . .'

'Where,' she asked calmly, 'where are you taking me, Antoine?'

He coloured. 'Well, we can go to a hotel first. Till we get the legal things sorted out, and then . . .'

Kate laughed and stood up. 'And then you'll take me to the château. And we'll live happily ever after. You, me and your mother. Is that what you have in mind, Antoine?'

'Something like that, Kate. I don't blame you for

being angry, *chérie* . . .'

'Angry?' Kate gave a light mocking laugh. 'You underestimate the power you had, Antoine. Angry scarcely describes the feeling I had when I found out what had happened. Wicked is how I would describe what you did to me.' Her voice trembled and she bit her lip fiercely. 'You, who had said you loved me, who should have wanted to protect me . . .'

'But Charles was there to look after you.' Antoine turned to look appealingly at his cousin. 'I knew that I could trust Charles. I've always relied on him. And you can't say that he hasn't cared for you, protected you.'

'It was you I wanted, Antoine.' Kate stared into the bewildered young face, refusing to look beyond him to that other dark figure.

'But now, Kate, we can surely forget?' Appealingly his hand came out to touch hers. 'We've got the rest of our lives.'

'No, Antoine,' now Kate was completely steady and confident, 'that's just what we don't have. You see, what you did was something I can never forget, or forgive. You shouldn't expect it.'

'Charles . . .' It was an appeal for help to an older brother.

'Kate's right, Antoine. Besides, there are other considerations now.' Charles's eyes were on Kate as he spoke and she had to struggle to resist her inclination to look at him.

'Other considerations?'

'Yes—you see, Antoine, for you I was prepared to do this absurd thing, to try to make you resist the domination of your mother. As Kate has said, we were both wrong and cruel to her. But I did it, and if there are any consequences I am prepared to face them. But what I'm trying to tell you, Antoine, is that although I was prepared to marry Kate for you, I'm not prepared to give her up for you.'

Kate hardly heard what he said. All she knew was that if she didn't escape from this room soon she would be forced to look at Charles, and that she knew she could not bear.

'Goodbye, Antoine.' She stared up into his face. 'Please don't try to see me again. Believe me, it will do no good.'

'Kate!' It was an anguished despairing cry.

'I don't want to see you again,' her self-control was rapidly disintegrating, 'nor ever to hear your name.' She put her hands over her ears and ran out of the room. 'It's a name I loathe!'

But strangely, when she reached her bedroom, a terrible calm enveloped her. She went along to the lumber room at the end of the corridor where her suitcases had been stacked and began, methodically, carefully, to take the clothes from her wardrobe and fold them. Her mind was full of practical details about what lay ahead of her. Could she get a train to Paris? Would the airline accept travellers' cheques for her air fare? Would she be best to stay in a hotel and make the journey tomorrow? Nevertheless at the back of her mind was the awful thought, like a painful blow over the heart, that soon she would have to say goodbye to Charles. If only she could remain calm. He might never know.

Then quite suddenly the door opened and he was standing there. The door closed and he leaned against the wall, his dark eyes following every deft move she made. Although her heart was hammering wildly Kate continued her precaution of avoiding looking directly at him. She picked up a pile of folded underwear and put it in the case on top of some skirts and jumpers.

'You seem remarkably incurious, Kate.' At last he spoke, and it was with a languid, almost amused voice.

'Yes.'

'You really don't want to know,' as he spoke he came over to stand close to her, supporting himself with one of the tall carved pillars at the foot of the bed, 'what has happened to Antoine?'

She shook her head briefly without speaking.

'You don't care that he left about half an hour ago, Kate?'

'I don't care.' But she did care that *he* had taken so long to come up to see her. To tell her what had happened. To find out if she needed any comfort.

'You're sure, Kate?' Suddenly his hands, strong as steel, came out and caught her by the shoulders, turning her round to face him so that there was no escaping the power of his possessive searching eyes. 'It's important to me to know.'

'Sure? Of course I'm sure.' Defensively she almost spat the words at him. 'I hate him. I hate you. Oh, why did I ever . . .' To her dismay all the tears she had been struggling against burst from her, she felt herself folded against his chest, felt his hands caressing her hair.

'Hush! Hush, my Kate. It doesn't matter.' Then he spoke in his own language, little murmured endearments which she had rejoiced in the previous night. At last her weeping eased and she pulled herself away from him.

'I'm sorry, I didn't mean to do that.' She tried to turn her tear-stained face from his, but he would have none of it, forcing her by means of a firm hand under her chin.

'If you really mean that you don't care, Kate, then I can tell you, explain a little so that perhaps you can understand why these things happened as they did. And why, dear Kate,' the tenderness in his voice made her tremble beneath his hands, but if he noticed he gave no sign. Instead the dark face became sombre while the eyes continued to search for she knew not what. 'Dear, dear Kate, I could not tell before what *you* surely had every right to know.'

He sighed, relaxing his hold, depriving her of the life-giving support of his arms. '*Ma tante*, Antoine's mother,' he continued in a voice now deprived of emotion, 'she is, as you must have realised, quite unbalanced.' Closely he watched until the merest inclination of her head signalled her acquiescence. 'I had not seen her for many years and although I had heard from Antoine how her possessive eccentricity had increased I had not appreciated just how mad she had become. I fear that at last Antoine must do something, it has gone too far to be ignored, for everyone's safety she must . . .' He broke off and there was a moment's silence before he continued. 'But these unpleasant truths I wished to keep from you, *ma petite*. I still thought—*mon Dieu*, how I tortured myself with the thought!—that you loved Antoine and would still wish to marry him.' He shrugged. 'I would not have you caused additional anxiety, thinking you were to join with a family so . . .' —he hesitated—'. . . so unstable.'

'Oh!' Wild thoughts were running through her head. She was remembering what Françoise had told her. Was it never to end, this nightmare? She heard the deep voice continuing, tried to concentrate her mind on the meaning of his words.

'Besides, there was also the possibility that Madame might do you some injury. If she had guessed or even suspected what was planned there's no knowing what action she might have taken. This obsession with the family, the line of the Savoney-Morlets, although it's all nonsense, she's completely ensnared in her own web. She and practically all those who imagine they owe their loyalty to the château.' His mouth was a grim line when he finished speaking and he stood looking down at Kate almost as if he didn't see her. Then he relaxed, his shoulders moved in a faint gesture of dismissal. 'Ah well, perhaps we should not judge her too harshly. She had some terrible experiences in the war. You know the hills and woods around the château were a centre for the Maquis and there was a terrible battle between them and the Germans in which Madame lost two cousins. *And* her brother, who was pursued to the house and shot down in front of her.' Without seeming to notice Kate's shiver he went on, 'There were rumours that they had been betrayed by a careless radio message from London. Since then . . .' again he shrugged, '. . . who knows, it might explain her fanatical love of France, her hatred for foreigners. Perhaps she was so before.'

There was a long silence when there seemed nothing to say, but in fact Kate had barely understood his explanations. Later the time would come for that, perhaps even for pity, but now her mind was occupied with other, more desolate thoughts. What more sensible, more natural for a man with the pride of the Savoney-Morlets than to ensure that any tainted blood, any suspect heredity should be frustrated, denied? A tiny protesting moan escaped her lips as she recognised that his long explanation did little except to confirm what she had been told.

But then his hands, beguiling, irresistible, came out again to catch hers, to pull her towards him. The beautiful eyes were shadowy with longing as she looked up into that beloved face, saw the lips frame words that she could hardly understand. 'Now all I want to know, Kate, is that you'll stay with me. Even though I know you hate the name of Savoney-Morlet. If you wish it, *ma petite*, then perhaps we can think of changing it. There is always Saint Cyr.'

But Kate hardly noticed his later words, all her thoughts were concentrated on his first words. 'You want me to stay here. To be your mistress . . .'

'Kate! Kate!' Shaking her very gently, he laughed down into her perplexed face. 'Kate, *ma petite*, you are my wife. Had you forgotten? However it came about that is the truth of the matter. And,' his face grew serious, intense, 'what happened last night, on that bed, was no casual encounter—not for you, not for me. It was something inevitable. No matter how I tried to assure you that it would not. My longing for you, these circumstances where you were my wife and yet I had none of a husband's privileges—all that was driving me mad. You see, Kate, that first moment when I raised the veil to look into your face, I knew that I had met the woman I wanted to be with for the rest of my life. Can you imagine the torment of it!' He shuddered and put a hand briefly to his eyes.

'Then it wasn't . . .' She bit her lip, unable to speak the words.

'What, my sweet . . .?'

Still she hesitated, remembering what Françoise had told her and remembering now with awful clarity Charles's reaction that day by the pool when he had thought she was pregnant. Could his anger have been a result of the frustration of his plans? She could bear the uncertainty no longer and the words tumbled from her mouth. 'Françoise told me you would go to any lengths to ensure that your son would inherit the château. Even if Antoine thought it was his son.'

He said a word Kate didn't understand but she knew that he was being uncomplimentary to Françoise. 'Do you believe that, Kate?'

'I . . . I don't know.'

'You ought to know.' The little sigh he gave told her he was disappointed. Then, 'But why do I say that? Why should you know what to believe after what you've been through? If I tell you that the thought had never crossed my mind would you believe me?'

'If you say so, Charles.' It was her turn to sigh just a little. 'But your aunt . . . You said . . . You and she . . . You said that you had agreed to marry me for a consideration.' Her eyes searched his face.

'Yes, Kate.' His expression was very sober as he answered. 'I told you that—and I'm sorry. There was a certain amount of truth in it. But when I told you, I was trying to remind myself of the original reasons for the marriage, the sense that I would be able to repay her by helping Antoine to break free. She did use a little bit of bribery as a means of persuading me and I pretended to take the bait. But afterwards, when I had seen you, Kate, and even more when I got to know you just a little, I felt ashamed of what I had done. But yet

I couldn't regret it. Never, never could I regret . . .'

'Oh, Charles!' Scarcely able to bear the suffusion of happiness that swept through her, she leaned her head against his chest, hearing just beneath her ear the firm steady beating of his heart. She spread her fingers wide on the smooth cotton shirt, feeling the muscular contours of his body. 'And Françoise...' It was almost the very last little query at the back of her mind, although it seemed supremely unimportant now.'...You and she?'

'She and I . . .' there was laughter in his voice as he paraphrased her words, '. . . never were what you were thinking. Her father was my best friend and I owe him a great deal, but that does *not* include taking on his daughter. He understood very well that she has serious problems and before he died he asked me to keep an eye on her. I've done that for the last five years, but now I think she's old enough to go her own way. Anyway, like most people she only takes the advice she wants to hear.'

'She's in love with you.'

'I doubt it. She likes changes, and as I've never had the inclination to be one of a long line of lovers she may feel frustrated. If I had been willing I'm sure she would have tired of me long ago.'

'And Auriol?' Some final little prick of jealousy made her mention the name of the beautiful model in the photograph downstairs. 'Were you and she . . .'

'Never.' His mouth came down and brushed the top of her head. 'Never, my sweet. I don't think her husband would have liked it.'

Her husband. It was strange that it had never occurred to Kate that Auriol might be married. And yet what could be more natural? She might have spared herself all those tortured jealous longings, about both Françoise and Auriol. She gave a little sigh and raised her face to his, her heart responding with a bound to the spark of knowing amusement she saw in his eyes. 'Charles, why? It's all been so strange, so incredible. Why? Why?'

'That I can't tell you, Kate. I can hardly forgive myself.' He shook his head and the dark eyes fringed with ridiculously long lashes lingered over her face. 'And yet if I hadn't we might never have met. Perhaps it was all deviously planned by fate to bring us together.' As he spoke his lips brushed against hers, tantalising, his hand moved to the tempestuous beat of her heart. Her arms crept round his neck, her long fingers entwined themselves in the dark hair, her lips parted beneath his searching, persuasive mouth.

'Kate.' It was a groan as his mouth moved along her cheek.

'Mmm!' She was too languorous with longing for him to speak.

'There's something more I have to tell you.' Her hands moving over his chest were all at once still, her voice faint with apprehension.

'Yes?'

'I have just been on the telephone—that is what took me so long. I've been speaking to your mother.'

'You . . . you've *what*?'

'I rang her to say that we are married. She and Andrew have been back in New York for nearly a week.' He held her away from him and his expression as he looked down at her was faintly reproving.

'Oh?'

'I told her that we would be flying out there very soon and that we would be going on to Bali, for a delayed honeymoon. I hope,' his voice was deep and tender, 'I hope, *ma petite*, that you'll agree to go with me.'

Kate smiled mysteriously as she looked up at him. 'Have I any choice?' she asked dreamily.

'Not really.' Charles's arms folded tightly about her. 'I believe neither of us has had any choice in what has happened. But now I think,' he spoke slowly while his eyes moved tantalisingly over her face, 'I think that the tidying up is going to have to wait just a little longer . . .' And his mouth came down towards hers with such fierce possessiveness that she melted willingly, pliantly against him. 'There are,' and his voice had grown husky with emotion, 'so many other exciting things to do. My Kate.'

We value your opinion...

You can help us make our books even better by completing and mailing this questionnaire. Please check [✓] the appropriate boxes.

1. Compared to romance series by other publishers, do Harlequin novels have any additional features that make them more attractive?

   1.1 ☐ yes   .2 ☐ no   .3 ☐ don't know

   If yes, what additional features? _____
   _____
   _____

2. How much do these additional features influence your purchasing of Harlequin novels?

   2.1 ☐ a great deal   .2 ☐ somewhat   .3 ☐ not at all   .4 ☐ not sure

3. Are there any other additional features you would like to include?
   _____
   _____
   _____

4. Where did you obtain this book?

   4.1 ☐ bookstore   .4 ☐ borrowed or traded
    .2 ☐ supermarket   .5 ☐ subscription
    .3 ☐ other store   .6 ☐ other (please specify)_____

5. How long have you been reading Harlequin novels?

   5.1 ☐ less than 3 months   .4 ☐ 1-3 years
    .2 ☐ 3-6 months   .5 ☐ more than 3 years
    .3 ☐ 7-11 months   .6 ☐ don't remember

6. Please indicate your age group.

   6.1 ☐ younger than 18   .3 ☐ 25-34   .5 ☐ 50 or older
    .2 ☐ 18-24   .4 ☐ 35-49

Please mail to: Harlequin Reader Service

In U.S.A.	In Canada
1440 South Priest Drive	649 Ontario Street
Tempe, AZ 85281	Stratford, Ontario N5A 6W2

Thank you very much for your cooperation.